FORBIDDEN
HAWAIIAN
NIGHTS

FORBIDDEN HAWAIIAN NIGHTS

CATHY WILLIAMS

MILLS & BOON

First published in Great Britain 2021
by Mills & Boon, an imprint of HarperCollins*Publishers* Ltd,
1 London Bridge Street, London, SE1 9GF

www.harpercollins.co.uk

HarperCollins*Publishers*
1st Floor, Watermarque Building,
Ringsend Road, Dublin 4, Ireland

Large Print edition 2021

Forbidden Hawaiian Nights © 2021 Cathy Williams

ISBN: 978-0-263-28859-9

05/21

MIX
Paper from
responsible sources
FSC® C007454

Printed and bound in Great Britain
by CPI Group (UK) Ltd, Croydon, CR0 4YY

To my treasured kids
and supportive partner, David.

CHAPTER ONE

MAX STOWE LISTENED to his brother's voice down the end of a telephone line thousands of miles away and did his utmost not to cut short the placatory monologue, which was designed to defuse the situation but was having the opposite effect.

James was currently in Dubai, dealing with the final nuts and bolts of the state-of-the-art eco-super-yacht they had commissioned to be hand-built a little over a year ago.

He, on the other hand, was here, staring out from the balcony of his hotel at a long strip of beach, mentally working out the approach he would take to discover the whereabouts of their wayward sister, who had done a midnight flit with only a brief goodbye and 'Don't worry about me' delivered via text message.

Who, Max wondered, had got the better deal?

Jaw clenched, handsome features rigid with the simmering tension that had had ample time to build on the long and exhausting flight to Hawaii, he cut short the conversation and slipped his mobile back into his trouser pocket.

The glorious view was completely lost on him. He had already had a shower but out here, standing on the broad balcony, he was still baking hot and uncomfortable.

And he was in a foul mood.

Under any other circumstances, heads would have rolled for this. He was as fair as the next man, but you didn't get to be at the top of the food chain by accepting incompetence and unreliability.

Unfortunately, these were far from normal circumstances, and with a sigh of frustrated resignation he spun round and headed back into the coldly air-conditioned penthouse suite of the five-star hotel.

Izzy. His sister. Where the hell was she? He knew where she *wasn't* and that was here, in

Hawaii, doing what she was being paid hand-somely to do.

Max refused to succumb to dark thoughts and alarming hypothetical scenarios. He was a man finely honed when it came to dealing with facts and adept at finding solutions to problems as they arose. Izzy's disappearance was simply a problem and he intended to find a solution to it. He knew exactly what road he was going to take to get where he wanted to go.

He glanced at his watch. It was four-thirty. The sun was beginning to dip outside, even though the heat continued unabated. On that beach, somewhere, lay the answer to this sit-uation in the form of one Mia Kaiwi, age twenty-seven, height five-six, occupation landscape gardener and jack-of-all-trades at the boutique hotel he was currently having built on Oahu.

Two days ago, he had received his sister's text. Two days ago, he had communicated with Nat, the foreman in charge of the proj-ect, to find out what the hell was happening. And two days ago he had found out that, while neither Nat nor his sidekick Kahale seemed to have the foggiest idea where his sister had gone, her close friend, Mia, would.

It had taken him twenty-four hours to close various deals he couldn't possibly leave half finished. During that time, Max had resisted the temptation to get one of his people to track his sister down. It would have been easy enough, but he would wait until he could confront the best friend and get the information he needed from that source himself.

Weighing in with a heavy hand might win the battle but it wasn't going to win the war.

But, hell, this was the last place he wanted to be—waiting for five o'clock to roll round so that he could walk the crowded strip of beach in search of some woman he didn't know. A woman who, according to Nat, would reliably be found teaching surf lessons to kids, which was what she did like clockwork every Saturday afternoon between three and five.

He'd given orders that she was not to be

alerted to his arrival. No time to do a runner or to rehearse any non-answers to his questions. No, he intended to surprise the woman into telling him what he wanted to know. Once he'd done that, he would allow himself the grand total of four days to sort out this thorny and inconvenient business so that he could return to London to pick up where he had left off with his fast paced, no-time-to-breathe life.

He would unearth his sister from wherever she was hiding, find out what the hell was going on, remind her of the easy ride she had been given—even if he had to write it down for her in bullet points—and get her back on track.

And he would do it in as non-judgemental a manner as he could possibly muster, even though he was genuinely having a hard time grasping her immaturity at taking off without warning.

Fifteen minutes later, he hit the beach at an easy pace. He'd packed the bare minimum of clothes because he anticipated a speedy return to London. Shorts had not featured. He possessed none. Right now, as he began strolling along the long and extremely crowded arc of sand, he was beginning to regret the lack of them because he was sweltering, even though the sun was beginning to set with dramatic splendour.

He walked slowly, eyes narrowed, missing nothing. The beach was emptying out and it was more beautiful than he had first thought. The ocean was darkening from rich turquoise to deep navy and the buildings behind him, of which his hotel was one, were beginning to twinkle as lights were switched on.

The air was filled with voices, bursts of laughter and the revving of motorbike engines.

And then there she was. Unmissable, as Nat had said. She was stacking surfboards, her movements fast and graceful, and she was so slender that she looked as though a puff of wind might blow her over. Her hair was tied up in a ponytail and she was surrounded by a bunch of excited kids. *Surf for Kids*. The sign was almost obscured by the upright arrangement of surfboards.

She was laughing and barefoot, wearing a bikini top and a sarong that dipped just below her belly button. When the last of the kids was led away she immediately slipped on a baggy tee shirt, consulted the over-sized watch on her wrist and began heading away, having roped the surfboards together and padlocked them.

Max quickened his pace. He was here to do a job and, the quicker the job got done, the quicker he would be able to leave.

Mia sensed Max behind her with a sort of sixth sense she had developed over the years. She had become accustomed to blowing off men who tried to chat her up. Here on the beach blowing off men was as irritating as swatting flies and she wasn't in the mood for it. She was *never* in the mood for it, and she *particularly* wasn't in the mood for it this evening.

She spun round without warning and stood

back, arms folded, determined to give whoever it was a piece of her mind.

Her eyes travelled from the bottom up.
From loafers and long silver-grey chinos, to
the white polo shirt with the tiny black logo
on the pocket, and up, up until her brown
eyes collided with eyes very much the colour
of the ocean as it was now—deep, dark and
fringed with the thickest of lashes she had
ever seen on a man.

The man was stupidly, sinfully drop-dead
gorgeous, from the perfectly sculpted, lean
features to the imposing beauty of his mus-
cled body, which not even his idiotically inappropriate clothing could conceal.

The guy oozed sex appeal and Mia was so
taken aback that she could only stare for a
few addled, frozen seconds.

She recovered fast from the temporary
lapse.

'Forget it.' She turned around and quickly
began walking away, head held high, backbone straight, her body language informing

whoever the guy was that she wasn't on the market for any kind of casual pick-up.

'Come again?'

His voice was dark, smooth and velvety. Mia didn't stop to look around, but she felt the hairs on the back of her neck stand on end.

'You heard me,' she snapped, spinning round again and then taking a step back, because he was just so damned *tall,* his presence just so damned *overpowering.* 'I'm not interested. I don't want to have a drink with you. I don't want to go to a club with you. I don't want to have dinner with you.'

'I don't believe I asked you to do any of those things.'

Mia heard the coolness in his voice and was taken aback. There was a stillness about him and a feeling of complete self-control that she found a little disconcerting.

Who the heck was he?

The mere fact that the question had the temerity to pop into her head annoyed her.

Mia knew, without a trace of vanity, that

she drew looks. She was five-six and slender, with a heart-shaped face and full lips that turned heads. She was olive-skinned by birth, but a lifetime of living and working in the sun had deepened her natural colouring, and she was now a rich bronze with long, dark hair and caramel eyes.

So what if men looked? None of them got to her. After Kai, she had retreated from the dismal, soul-destroying business of looking for love. Her short marriage had been a slow and illuminating process of disillusionment. You go through that, she figured, and you were a fool not to learn from the experience.

She'd learnt.

'I'm not having this conversation,' she said, her coolness a match for his.

'Mia Kaiwi? That *is* your name, isn't it?'

Mia froze on the spot. This time, a thread of apprehension raced through her. She turned slowly to find that he was standing quite still, his head tilted to one side, his expression shuttered.

'Who the hell are you?'

'I'll tell you who I'm *not*,' Max said silkily. 'And that's someone looking for a pick-up.'

'How do you know my name?'

'Is there somewhere we can go to talk?'

'I'm not going anywhere with you.'

How did the guy know her name? Was he a dad to one of the kids in her surfing group?

No, of course he wasn't. You didn't forget a face like that, and Mia had never seen him in her life before.

Even on a beach where most of the guys were in shorts, and many of them young, good-looking and at the very peak of their fitness, this guy attracted attention. She was aware of people walking past, looking once and then looking again. He didn't seem to notice or, if he did, he didn't care.

'Oh, but you are.' Max paused. 'Now...' He looked around. 'Is there somewhere quiet around here? I would suggest my hotel, but as you seem to be under the mistaken impression that I'm about to make a pass at you I don't suppose that would be appropriate.'

'I could call someone to have you arrested,'

Mia said, but she was beginning to get the feeling that she was on shaky ground, because there was a self-assurance in the man that was unsettling.

'I wouldn't do that.' Max indicated a café further along the beach. It was a little busy, but they would be able to sit without people jostling them. 'There will do.'

Mia's mouth dropped open as he coolly began walking away, expecting her to follow.

Heart pounding and head beginning to throb with nervous tension, she found herself snapping out of her daze, tripping behind him to the café. At least she knew the owner at this place, so there was no way he could do anything to her.

Although, would he?

She was beginning to think that she had read the situation wrong, even though she couldn't work out what the alternative could be. He glanced over his shoulder to her and then stopped so that she could catch him up.

He must be at least six-three, she thought faintly. He seemed to tower over everyone in the café. Out of the corner of her eye she saw Mack, the owner, and his wife Rae, and she nodded. The café was only just beginning to fill up with another wave of people arriving at the beach. The families had left and all the twenty- and thirty-somethings would be heading down to have dinner at one of the food trucks that lined the strip of road at the back, or else just hang out in groups on the sand.

'Don't worry,' he drawled, looking down at her. 'Your friends will make sure you don't get kidnapped by me.'

'My friends?'

He nodded to the counter. 'I'm guessing you know those two behind. Good. If I can't reassure you that I'm not about to take advantage of you, then the presence of those two should.'

'I would be reassured if you actually told me your name,' Mia returned without batting an eye. 'You know mine, so it's only polite.'

'And I will. What do you want to drink?'

'A glass of water would be fine.'

The man shrugged. There were empty tables to choose from and he opted for one to the side of the café and away from the window.

'Everything okay, Mi?'

Mia forced herself to smile at Rae, an attractive woman with cropped blonde hair and an easy smile who had approached them with a pad and a pen. Right now, there was a question in her eyes, and Mia couldn't blame her. She had spent long enough joking that the next time Mia came to the café she wanted to see her with a nice young man. That hadn't happened yet so her curiosity would be spiked by the sight of Mia with the man semi sprawled in the chair opposite her, their knees practically touching, because the wooden table was tiny.

'Sure!' They ordered their drinks and Rae left them alone.

'Is it always like this?'

'What do you mean?' He had a voice that was lazy, only mildly interested, and yet strangely commanding. She was momentarily distracted by his direct gaze. Something about him was mesmerising and she wasn't quite sure why. Surely it couldn't be just a matter of good looks?

'Recognised wherever you go...'

'I've lived here all my life, and it's not enormous—not when so much of my time is spent on this beach. I teach the kids on a Saturday and a Sunday. I surf whenever I can. It can be a tight-knit community. And you still haven't told me your name.'

'Max Stowe. I'm Izzy's brother.'

Mia went very still.

That was the last thing she'd expected to hear even though she hadn't had a clue what she *had* been expecting.

He looked *nothing* like Izzy. Izzy was small and blonde with big, blue eyes.

This guy was a six-foot-something hunk with black hair and dark blue eyes and *Danger, Keep Away* stamped all over him.

She was still floundering in stunned silence when he pulled out a wallet and extracted a card which he shoved on the table between them.

His driving licence.

'Just in case you still have any doubts,' he drawled.

Mia didn't answer. She pushed the driving licence back towards him. 'I didn't realise you would be coming over,' she stammered.

'No,' Max soothed. 'I made sure to warn Nat and his assistant to keep my arrival under wraps.'

'Why?'

'I didn't want you to get any time to work out how you might avoid my questions.'

'What questions?' Mia asked. It still wasn't sinking in. *Izzy's brother?*

Izzy had mentioned Max in passing. 'Bossy' had been the term most frequently used when it came to a description.

Over five months as they had become firm friends, Mia had gleaned a picture of some-one who lived for work and ruled his much younger sister with an iron fist. An auto-cratic, humourless bore with a God complex.

Sitting here now, she was inclined to believe every aspect of that picture that had been painted in not so many words.

Hackles rising, she linked her fingers on the table and looked at him without flinching. He might be able to bully Izzy but there was no way he was going to bully *her*.

It took a lot of will power to maintain eye contact, and she had to yank herself back from the feeling that she was sinking into the depths of his steady, veiled, darkly mesmerising gaze…that somehow he had the power to scramble her brains.

'Where is she, Mia?' he asked softly.

He leaned towards her and she automatically leaned back to create distance between them.

'I don't know,' she said quickly, too quickly, because instead of thinking about her denial he smiled very slowly.

'Nice try, but I'm not buying it.'

'What makes you think that I know where Izzy is?'

'For a start, you're her close friend, and close friends confide. My sister would never have disappeared without telling someone where she was going. She certainly hasn't said a word to either myself or her brother and Nat is as much in the dark as I am, which really only leaves you.' He had ordered one of the local beers, and after Rae deposited their drinks on the table he tilted the bottle to his mouth, although his eyes never left her face, not for a second. He took his time drinking and then he lowered the bottle and broke the lengthening silence between them.

'Secondly,' he carried on, as though there had been no interruption to what he had been saying, 'your face is giving the game away. You know where she is, and I need to find her.'

'Don't think,' she said coldly, 'that you can bully me into telling you anything I don't want to.'

'And don't forget you work for me.'

Mia gasped. Yes—she worked for him! Of course, the second he had revealed his identity she had subliminally joined the dots, but on some other level she had not consciously registered that she was his employee.

She was registering it now and working out just what that involved.

As a landscape gardener, she had worked for herself for the past five years and had made a good enough living, but this was the first really big job she had ever taken on. And, more than that, she had found herself doing much more than the landscape gardening for the hotel and she enjoyed the additional responsibilities.

She enjoyed liaising with some of the suppliers, sorting out invoices when Izzy had too much on and, after the whole business of Jefferson and the effect he had had on Izzy, she had stepped up to the plate and got involved in most aspects of the business.

And she had been compensated financially for her efforts.

She knew that Max remotely controlled everything, so she knew that he would be well aware of her various responsibilities, and the fact that her pay cheque had been bumped up twice since she had started working for him.

What he wouldn't know was that she had used that money to get a bank loan to cover some vital repair work on her house. It was a loan that would have to be repaid.

She felt the heavy thudding of her heart as she belatedly recognised the consequences of having her pay stopped for whatever reason.

She would survive, but it would be tough, and she would have to go cap in hand to her parents for help, which was something she was loath to do.

Furthermore, she had been planning on this job leading to bigger and better things.

Word of mouth could be a powerful tool when it came to getting business in these parts. Were she to move on to bigger jobs—landscaping for hotels or offices—then she would be operating in a much bigger ball park and she could really see her earnings multiply.

But for that to happen she would need a damned good reference.

And where was that reference going to come from? The very guy staring at her now with brooding intensity, waiting for her to spill the beans.

'Are you *blackmailing* me?' she asked. She licked her lips and knew that she probably looked as nervous as she felt.

Max shrugged by way of response and sat back, his body language indicating someone utterly at ease with the situation.

No wonder Izzy had launched into a degree she didn't enjoy after her brother Max had proclaimed a business degree to be the best thing she could do, Mia thought. And she had hated it. He had probably used the same intimidating tactics on his sister that he was using on her now!

'I'm suggesting a fair exchange,' he countered. He didn't add to that, instead finishing his beer, giving her time to absorb the situation between them.

Mia thought of the work that had been done on her place, the loan she was repaying, the necessity of the job and the pay cheque she got at the end of the month.

'If Izzy wanted you to know where she was, don't you think she would have told you?' she asked, equivocating.

'Possibly,' Max returned, unruffled, 'but the fact remains that she didn't, hence why I am here. Tell me what I need to know, I will leave and life carries on uninterrupted for us both.'

'And what would you do if you do chase after her? Drag her back here kicking and screaming?'

He burst out laughing but there was little humour in his laughter. 'You have a vivid imagination, Mia.'

Mia looked down. She could feel his eyes boring into her and she wanted to fidget, restless and hyper-conscious of his presence opposite her.

She sneaked a glance from under her lashes and breathed in sharply, all her senses unfairly assailed by his sheer *beauty*.

His fingers were lightly circling the empty

beer bottle. Long fingers, strong forearms, a study in power in repose.

Her breathing slowed, and she was glad she was sitting down, because every part of her body suddenly felt wobbly.

'Has it occurred to you that I might be concerned for my sister's welfare?'

Mia looked at him fully and noted the underlying anxiety in his eyes. She hadn't noticed that before but then, she was ashamed to admit, she had been busy making sure to pigeonhole him and not give him the benefit of the doubt.

'What do you mean?'

'What do you think I mean?' he asked coldly. 'My brother and I got the same text from Izzy, along the lines that things were a bit tough for her at the moment, so she would be taking some time out, but that Nat and Kahale would be fine to pick up the slack. What do you think went through my head when I read that my sister was going through "a tough time"?'

He leaned forward, his dark features deadly

serious. 'I have no intention of playing games with you when Izzy may be in trouble. Whatever you think you're protecting her from, you're not doing her any favours, and if I have to force you into telling me her whereabouts then, believe me, I won't hesitate.'

'There's no need to threaten me!' Mia bristled with righteous indignation, but then sighed, because she could see how easily he might have jumped to all the wrong conclusions.

She knew that this project was his private indulgence. Izzy had let that fact slip after a couple of drinks shortly after they had started socialising, having the occasional meal together when they'd finished work. She'd been on her own, newly arrived, and Mia had enjoyed taking her under her wing. They'd hit it off.

'I know I should be grateful,' Izzy had confided with a hint of shame, 'and I am... I really *am*...but sorting out supplies and invoices and accounts and dealing with bank managers... It's just not *me*.'

Was this intimidating guy sitting opposite her aware of any of that?

And, if he wasn't, then what must be going through his head? He must be frantic with worry about whatever *tough times* he thought his sister might be facing.

'I don't intend to tell you where Izzy is,' she said firmly, but with sympathy in her voice. 'But I can assure you that there's no need for you to worry.'

'Really. What a relief. I'll leave now, shall I?'

'There's no need to be sarcastic.'

Odious, Mia thought. *Odious and rude and arrogant and a million other things I dislike in a man.*

She was mystified by her physical response to this man when her intellectual response to him was so negative. Was it because his looks were so compelling? Surely not? She couldn't be that shallow, could she? Or maybe it was because she had locked herself away behind a wall of ice after her brief, failed marriage to Kai. She and Kai had been kids when they'd married, and neither of them had expected their marriage to last only a mere year and a half because, on paper, the marriage had made complete sense.

Their families had known one another, they'd been childhood sweethearts and they'd both wanted to start their own families as soon as they could, just like their siblings had. Their lives had been mapped out and they had both rather liked the look of the map.

But it was not to be.

Their divorce had been amicable, but lessons had been learnt, and she had sealed herself off from men. But that had been four years ago! In her head, she'd envisaged herself marrying again. Of course she had. But this time she'd compiled a mental checklist of the perfect guy and she had no intention of deviating.

Was this puzzling reaction to Max Stowe simply her body reminding her that she wasn't quite as frozen in ice as she'd thought she was?

There was nothing about the guy she liked, yet his blue eyes on her made her feel hot and bothered, and *aware* with every pore in her body.

Had her withdrawal from the opposite sex simply not protected her enough from the sort of devastating effect this level of superb good looks could have on her? Was that it? He made her feel wildly out of her comfort zone when it came to men. No one she knew or had ever known was like this guy.

Some of her nerves eased as she rational-ised her reactions. She also could not let her-self forget that he was also her boss, and in his hands lay the power to make or break her.

She would have to temper her responses, she thought. She was going to have to act like an adult and be as cool, collected and self-assured as he was.

Or, at any rate, she was going to have to try.

Without betraying her friend's confidences.

'You do realise,' Max said, 'that, whilst it would be preferable not to involve a private investigator to handle this situation—which is something I'd hoped to avoid by approaching you directly—that remains an option.'

'She's not in any…trouble.' Mia grudgingly gave way. 'I mean, just in case you're thinking that she might have become involved in anything…dangerous.'

'Define *dangerous*.'

Mia looked at him. He was so…*self-controlled*. She could understand now how Izzy had managed to find herself in a place where she would rather not have been, in a job that did not cater for her creativity. Max Stowe exuded the aura of someone who didn't brook too much disagreement, someone who expected orders to be obeyed.

'She's not into drugs,' Mia said bluntly. 'And she hasn't done anything illegal. Not at all. You should know that. You're her brother.'

She was surprised at the dark flush that appeared on his high cheekbones.

'There is a considerable age difference between us,' he returned stiffly. 'Twelve years. Our relationship is possibly a little more formal than you might expect.'

'Why is that?' Mia heard herself ask.

Max looked at her with thinly veiled incredulity, and she was surprised to realise that she had overstepped the boundaries with that simple, innocuous question.

'None of my business.' She shrugged and he nodded curtly in agreement.

'No. It's not. You refuse to tell me the whereabouts of my sister. You think it's enough for you to say that she is not in a dangerous situation. Why should I believe you?'

'Because I'm telling the truth. I wish I could tell you why your sister needed a bit of space, but it would be breaking a confidence. All I can say is that she doesn't plan on staying away for ever.'

'There are no problems I would not be able to handle,' Max said flatly, his cold, deep voice oozing such supreme self-confidence that Mia's mouth fell open. 'Izzy should know that. When it comes to sorting things out, I have never let either her or my brother down.'

Mia clicked her tongue impatiently and wondered how someone evidently so astute could also be so dense. She raised her eyebrows but remained silent until he said irritably, 'If you have something to say, then I suggest you just go ahead and say it.'

'I got the impression that you're not that keen on people speaking their minds,' Mia murmured.

'It's strange because, if that's the impression you have about me, then you're obviously undeterred by it,' he returned bluntly, and she blushed.

'Izzy doesn't want you *sorting her out,*' she confessed. 'She hasn't just taken time out— she specifically asked me to make sure you didn't try and locate her. She wants a bit of time and you'd be making a big mistake, in my opinion, if you didn't give it to her...'

CHAPTER TWO

'SHE SPECIFICALLY ASKED YOU…to make sure I didn't follow her…?'

Frustration, bewilderment and something else tore through him, something ill-defined that pressed uncomfortably behind his ribcage.

He had done his utmost for his siblings. When their parents had died twelve years ago, Izzy had been just ten and he had been twenty-two, the same age she was now. Young and fresh out of university, ready to spread his wings. Fate had had other plans in store. His parents had been killed in their light aeroplane, which they had insisted on taking out despite poor weather conditions.

In a heartbeat, Max had found himself catapulted out of his youth and into instant, responsible adulthood. It had fallen to him to become caretaker to both his siblings and he had done so without complaint. He had done his utmost to make sure that their lives remained as steady as possible whilst he had put every thought he had ever vaguely had of taking time out on permanent hold.

Of course it had helped that his parents, both wealthy in their own right, had left behind a company in reasonably good health, thanks to delegation. Because his father, from memory, had never graced the inside of his office as he'd spent most of his time having fun.

Truthfully, Max had never surfaced from the weight of having to provide for his younger siblings.

And now his sister…didn't want him finding her?

He had made sure to take care of her! He had guided her through her life choices and arranged this job for her here! How many girls fresh out of university were given the golden opportunity to use their business degree to set up a boutique hotel in Hawaii with only a few guidelines and minimal supervision, free to make their own mark and prove their worth?

'That's ridiculous,' he asserted with a dismissive wave of his hand. 'I could do with another drink. And something to eat.' He beckoned someone across without taking his eyes off her.

The café was filling up. In her baggy tee shirt and sarong and flip-flops, she should have stood out, but in fact everyone else seemed to be wearing the same casual uniform. He tugged at the collar of his polo shirt, uncomfortably hot under the sultry overhead fan.

'Why is it ridiculous?'

'Exactly what did my sister tell you? Are you going to stick with water? Refuse the offer of food?'

Mia glanced briefly at the plastic menu Rae had brought over, but actually she knew what was on offer without having to consult any menu, and she ordered a Maui lager and a plate of Korean barbecue wings. She was hungry, and why not?

'Izzy knew that you would want to find her.'

'Hardly a surprise.'

'She…'

'What? She *what*?' Max stifled his impatience. For someone so adept at speaking her mind, she now seemed reluctant to expand on what she had said.

He watched her with brooding eyes, noting the flush in her cheeks and the fact that she couldn't quite look him in the eye. She might be outspoken to the point of annoying—and she might go against the grain, because nearly every woman he met made it their duty to engage his interest—but she was truly exquisite to look at, with her flawless brown skin and expressive eyes.

He shifted uncomfortably and frowned as his libido responded in a way that was utterly inappropriate.

He reminded himself that he was sitting here with this woman for one reason and one reason only. To locate his sister. It was proving more tedious than anticipated but Max had no doubt that he would get the information he wanted sooner rather than later. He had to because he had meetings scheduled and he had no intention of bailing on any of them.

'Look...' Drinks had arrived, beer for both of them, and he cradled his ice-cold bottle for a few seconds before tipping some down. 'I'm not in the mood for playing games. I'm on a tight timetable here. I haven't got time to try and coax answers out of you.'

'Izzy specifically doesn't want you to bring her back. She needs to clear her head. She... she had a bit of a relationship with a guy and it didn't go according to plan.'

Max stilled. He linked his fingers on the table and stared at her. 'Talk to me.'

'I shouldn't have said as much as I did, but honestly, Izzy just needs time to recover.'

'What happened?'

'Nothing happened! That's just it. Nothing at all happened and I think Izzy hoped that something might. That something serious might happen.'

'Who is he?'

Max banked down a surge of anger at whoever the guy was who was responsible for his sister's hasty disappearance. All the protective instincts that had been in place inside him for so many years raced to the surface and he clenched his fists, breathing deeply.

'It doesn't matter who he is,' Mia murmured.

Their eyes met, his dark with rage, hers calm and unruffled, and he felt himself relax a little.

'I'm finding it hard to imagine my sister involved with a scumbag,' he growled.

'Maybe,' Mia said under her breath, 'you're finding it hard to imagine your sister with *anyone*.'

Mia sat back, realising that she hadn't touched her beer, but then every ounce of her attention had been focused on the guy sitting opposite her.

He emanated such simmering power and

restless energy that she was oblivious to her surroundings.

Their food was being brought to them now, and she drank some of the beer and hesitantly began picking at the food, trying hard to marshal her thoughts.

Should she have betrayed that confidence? Should she have mentioned the business between Izzy and Jefferson?

But how else could she have deterred Max from doing what he had threatened to do? Why would he have believed anything else she'd told him? He didn't know her. And if he didn't believe her then what would stop him from hiring a PI to hunt down Izzy? He was rich, so that was something he could easily accomplish with a single phone call.

She knew Izzy well enough to suspect that if her brother hounded her down their relationship would take a battering.

Even so...

She dropped her eyes and tried to enjoy some of the fantastic barbecue on her plate, but her heart was pounding, and her head was beginning to throb with stress.

'What do you mean by that?'

'Sometimes you have to stand back and let the people you care about make whatever mistakes they have to make.'

'I gather from that remark that you and my sister have shared lots of cosy chats together? Izzy has never, *never,* given the slightest hint that she finds me over-protective.'

'Well, you asked me why she disappeared, and I've told you. There's nothing more I'm going to add to that.' She shoved her plate away and wiped her fingers on the damp tissues that had come with the wings.

He had worked his way through a couple of beers and a generous helping of *poke*. He'd managed to get some on his expensive polo shirt and that small detail made him seem much more human, much less forbidding.

He might be tough and ruthless, and downright arrogant in his assumption that getting exactly what he wanted was his right, but he was also human, and she wondered what it must feel like for him to be told that the sister he had spent years caretaking no longer needed to be looked after.

Mia knew about their unusual and unhappy background. Not in any great detail, but enough.

She had felt sorry for Izzy. She had had a very clear idea of what her brother was like. Driven, ambitious, *stifling*. But she had never met him before today, and it was easy to form opinions of people based on what was said about them. Indeed, it was impossible *not* to.

She'd sympathised hugely with her friend. She couldn't envisage a life without the support of parents, or the laughter of a jostling, rowdy household. It was what she had grown up with. Four sisters, nephews and nieces all meeting up as often as they possibly could because they enjoyed their times together. No family was ever without its problems, because such was the nature of life, but she just couldn't imagine the sadness of the sort of silent life her friend seemed to have had.

'I'm sorry.' She interrupted the growing silence and he scowled.

'For what?'

'It can't be easy learning that your sister doesn't want you to…follow her…'

'Thanks for the show of sympathy.' Max looked away, jaw clenched. 'But I'll cope.'

'If you choose to get someone involved to find Izzy, then I can't stop you,' Mia said. 'But I don't think that would be such a great idea.'

'What happened with that man? Was violence involved?'

'Good heavens, *no!*' Mia said, startled. 'You don't have to worry on that score *at all.* Jefferson was an idiot, that's all.' She sensed rather than saw the passing shadow of intense relief lighten his lean, handsome face.

She awkwardly offered to settle half the bill, and for the first time, when he looked at her, it was without the cool remoteness that had sent chills down her spine. When his eyes rested on her this time, they were a little bit startled, a little bit amused.

'I can count on the fingers of one hand,' he murmured, 'the number of women who have ever offered to do that. No—scratch that. I have never been in the company of *any* woman who has ever offered to pick up her share of the bill, so thank you for the offer.'

Mia blushed. Her skin tingled and she was aware of something else that had crept into the conversation, something that didn't threaten and didn't make her hackles rise, and that something sent a shiver racing up and down her spine.

'Well, *I* always make sure to pay my half whenever I go out with a guy,' she countered briskly.

'And I expect those occasions happen frequently?'

Mia's blush deepened. Suddenly, she felt out of her depth. Since Kai, she had been on a handful of dates, all of which had ended up in the 'just good friends' category.

She had not gone on any of those dates because she had really wanted to. All of them, all *five* of them, had been arranged by one of her sisters and Mia had politely gone along because she hadn't wanted to seem ungracious.

She was the odd one out in her family, the only one without a significant other. Two of her sisters were married with kids and the other two were engaged. She was twenty-seven years old and she knew what the unspoken commentary on her life was...

When is she going to settle down?

When will Mia get over her failed marriage, which was four years ago, and find herself a nice, decent guy...?

So when they'd arranged for her to meet one of those 'nice, decent guys', she had known they'd done so because they loved her, and the last thing she'd wanted to do was hurt their feelings.

'It's getting late,' she began, reaching for her backpack.

'I wouldn't dream of asking you to pay for a plate of chicken wings and a bottle of beer, incidentally,' he said with authority.

'In that case, thanks,' Mia returned awkwardly. 'Especially as I didn't give you the answer you wanted to hear. I'll head off now, if you don't mind. I'm going to have to tell Izzy that I've mentioned the business about Jefferson, and of course if she wants you to get in touch then I'll relay the message. Or she'll contact you herself. But if not...' She let the unspoken rider hover between them. If nothing was said, then Izzy didn't want his interference in her life.

'I'll walk out with you.' He stood up and dropped a handful of bills on the table, plenty to cover what they had eaten.

'It's okay.' Mia backed away and licked her lips. She felt ridiculous in her sarong, tee shirt and flip-flops, especially alongside him.

'Well...the truth is,' Max drawled, ignoring her protest and following her outside, where the air was balmy and the beach after a brief lull post families and small kids, was once again busy with young people hanging out in groups, 'we haven't quite finished this conversation.'

'What do you mean?' She looked at him

with alarm. 'Like I said, I can't stop you from—'

'Oh, I know what you said, and I agree.'

'Sorry?' She looked up at him, puzzled, and once again was overwhelmed by that weird, disconcerting force-field he seemed to emanate without even realising.

He cupped her elbow, moving her out of the way of a couple of kids jogging past, and that passing physical contact sent a jolt of awareness through her like a bolt of electricity.

He was escorting her away from the beach and towards the road that separated the coast from the metropolis.

Oahu, sometimes nicknamed the Heart of Hawaii, was the most metropolitan of the islands. Honolulu, the capital, boasted bars and restaurants and galleries and museums, and right now all those buildings formed a back-lit drop that stretched as far as the eye could see. This was as close as urban could get to coastal, man-made to nature, and at night it seemed even more impressive. The black ocean soothed while the frantic city thrilled.

The heat, the noise, the lively thrum of people, traffic and *life* never failed to give her a kick.

Right at the moment, however, it wasn't quite delivering on that front because she was way too conscious of the man walking beside her. He'd dropped his hand from her elbow but the place where he had touched continued to burn and she had to resist the temptation to rub it in the palm of her hand.

'My hotel.' He nodded. Mia knew that he would be staying at one of the most expensive hotels in the city, with views of the sea. She hoped that he didn't have plans to continue their conversation inside his hotel because if he did then she would have to put her foot down—not that she had any idea what more she could contribute anyway.

The thought of being inside a hotel with Max brought her out in a cold sweat because there was something intimate about the confines of a hotel.

'I'm afraid I really must get back home,'

she said in a prim, breathless voice, and Max laughed under his breath.

'There you go again,' he drawled as they crossed the busy ribbon of road and began heading into the city at an easy pace. 'Assuming the worst. I wasn't interested in chatting you up on the beach and I'm not trying to coerce you into the hotel with me.'

Mia was relieved he couldn't see the mortified flush that rushed into her cheeks. What must be going through his head? How big must he think her ego?

Her first reaction to him had been to assume that he was chatting her up, presumably because she thought herself *so* irresistible. Then that remark about all those numerous dates she'd gone on! She'd done nothing to dispel that inaccuracy because her private life was none of his business but even so...

And now here she was, assuming, as far as he was concerned, that he was trying to entice her back to his place.

The ironic thing was that Mia was very far

removed from having any kind of ego when it came to men.

No matter what she looked like, the bottom line was that her marriage had failed, and she'd realised long ago that, although she had surfaced from that brief and unsuccessful union, she still carried, deep inside her, a sense of personal failure that, because things hadn't worked out, she had misjudged a situation so badly. It had been her own secret shame.

So to have Max, or anyone, somehow thinking that she was full of herself couldn't be further from the truth!

There was no reason for her to defend herself, because his opinion didn't matter, but she still bristled at his misconceptions.

'I'm taking you to the hotel because it'll be easier for you to get a taxi back to your house from there.'

'I'm fine with public transport.'

'Do you *ever* concede anything without a full-blown argument? Are you like that with everyone you meet? I'm going to concede that you might be right about my sister. It's disappointing that Izzy is somehow afraid of talking to me about what's on her mind, but so be it.' He'd slowed down as they approached the hotel, with its dramatic columns and graceful, semi-circular marble frontage and sculpted trees guarded by a stiff and serious-looking official in uniform. As expected, there was a bank of taxis waiting outside.

He drew her to a stop and looked down at her. In the shadowy darkness of the night, his face was all sharp angles and, staring up at him, Mia felt her mouth go dry.

Was Izzy afraid to talk to him? She suddenly wanted to tell him that *afraid* wasn't quite the right term.

But, frankly, she was unable to get the words out because he took her breath away. Literally. She was having trouble remembering how to breathe.

'You tell me that she specifically does not want me to know her whereabouts. That being the case…and I'm going to take your word for it that a blip in her emotional life is the cause of this drama rather than anything more serious...'

'You shouldn't underestimate how awful heartbreak can be.'

Staring up at him with the sort of ridiculous fascination that annoyed her intensely but was somehow impossible to control, she realised that he didn't understand what she was talking about.

Yes, he had accepted that getting a private investigator involved to track Izzy down might not be the best option, and to all intents and purposes he had trusted Mia when she'd told him that Izzy hadn't rushed off because she had become involved in anything shady. But, judging from the cynical expression on his face, the notion of anyone tailoring their behaviour because of a broken heart made no sense to him at all.

Against her will, Mia felt a surge of curiosity.

He was so cold, so aloof...

So controlled.

Was he like that in every aspect of his

life? Had he never had a broken heart? She vaguely remembered Izzy once telling her that her brother was a workaholic. Did that mean that he had *no* time for relationships? Surely not…?

She imagined that there would be no end of women banging on his door begging to be allowed in, with him looking the way he did.

Her nostrils flared and a sudden heat coursed through her body. She was shocked to the core by the damp pooling of moisture between her legs.

'We'll have to agree to differ on that score,' Max was saying coolly.

Mia, eye level with his chest, was busy trying to ward off intrusive, inappropriate images of what he might look like under that polo shirt.

She heard herself grunt something noncommittal by way of response.

'Are you listening to what I'm saying?' Max demanded, and she reluctantly looked up at him and nodded.

'Yes, but I'm beginning to flag. I don't

know what else you want me to say about this. I feel terrible about breaking Izzy's confidence, but it was the only way I could think of to stop you from employing someone to find her. But now you know why she vanished, and now you know that she's going to be heading back, and I'm sure she'll be in touch within the next week. So what else is there for us to talk about?'

Max sighed and shot her a kindly and only mildly questioning look.

'Your status as my employee, of course...'

Mia stilled. How could she have let that slip her mind even for a moment? In her head, she had pictured herself heading back to her house never to lay eyes on him again. How naïve of her.

'Well, yes...'

'I hate to get between you and your beauty sleep, but this is going to be slightly more than a five-minute conversation, Mia. Of course, we can conduct it out here, with the passing traffic and beeping of horns interrupting us every two minutes, or we could actually go inside the hotel. To the bar. Where we would be able to sit and converse in relative comfort.' He paused, then added in a tone intended to make her hackles rise, 'Naturally, if you still feel wary about that situation, then we can remain standing out here. I will, of course, choose not to insist that we go inside.'

And there, in a nutshell, was the fist of steel inside the not-so-velvet glove, she thought. She worked for him and, like any boss, he was entitled to give orders. He'd managed to make that clear without actually saying so in so many words.

He'd also managed to remind her of the inaccurate picture of herself she had managed to paint. The implication was that there would be people around them so she could go ahead and feel safe that he wasn't going to do anything inappropriate because she was simply just too irresistible.

Mia ground her teeth together and clenched her fists and thought that she had never wanted to smack someone more.

'Sure.' She did her best to paint a casual smile on her face.

Max tilted his head to one side and was silent for a few seconds, then he nodded and began moving off towards the brightly lit, guarded entrance.

Infuriating man, she thought, following him into the hotel and feeling *really* under-dressed amongst the designer-clad tourists milling in groups.

The lobby was huge and dissected by four impressive marble columns. The white columns and the white walls were a stark contrast to the highly polished dark wood of the floors and the huge rugs, with their pale green leaf motifs that looked too expensive to walk on.

It reeked of opulence and she felt a kick of nerves as she walked alongside him, feeling self-conscious in her beach wear.

It was blessed relief to get to the relative dark sanctuary of the bar, with its bank of arched windows and its long, granite-topped bar behind which several beautiful young people were serving drinks. It was a huge space and very much conducive to conversations not being overheard.

Mia slid into a chair and, once orders had been taken, she leaned forward and linked her fingers on the table.

'You said you wanted to talk to me about my…my status as your employee. I know I didn't give you the answer you wanted to hear, but please tell me whether I still have a job.' Her voice was low and urgent. She was already trying to work out how she might supplement her income should she get the sack.

The landscaping job at the hotel was only in the very first stages but she had been thrilled by the size of the job, and the opportunities it offered to diversify her work, and she had given most of her attention over to it. It was also stupidly well-paid.

She blanched as she did the maths in her head about what would happen should she lose her income.

'Calm down.' He sat back as drinks were

placed in front of them along with two heavy glass dishes brimming with hot cashew nuts.

'How can I be calm? You were happy to blackmail me to get what you wanted.'

Max shrugged, unfazed by that accusation. 'All's fair in love and war. If I'd thought you were holding out on information that might have put my sister in jeopardy, then there's no doubt I would have been heavy handed in my dealings.' He paused to sip some of his drink. 'As it happens, I do believe what you've said, and I trust you haven't airbrushed the situation. Personally, I don't see why a disappointing personal relationship is reason enough to dump a dream job and leave the people around you in the lurch but, as I said, we'll have to agree to disagree on that point.'

Mia took heart from the fact that he hadn't yet issued her with her final papers. She still felt the need for some Dutch courage, though, so she sipped the cocktail she had ordered and helped herself to some of the nuts. It was late, and she was still hungry after her plate of chicken wings, which she had only picked at because her stomach had been too churned up with tension.

'Here's the thing, Mia,' he drawled. 'In Izzy's absence, I'm going to have to hang around here for a bit longer than I had anticipated.'

'Why?'

'Why do you think?' He shot her a quizzical look, as if encouraging her to arrive at what should be a glaringly obvious conclusion.

Mia refused to be cowed. 'Nat is brilliant,' she pointed out. 'So is Kahale. Plus, there's only a minimum of people on board at the moment because the hotel is only really just getting underway.'

She realised that she was propping herself up on her hands, so she breathed deeply and forced herself to relax. 'Workers are on board for the building side of things, and I know that there was a hold-up on some of the supplies, but that's been sorted now. We haven't got any of the actual fitters in at the moment because there's so much basic work still to be done. It's just a twenty-room hotel, though, so it shouldn't take for ever to sort out. Nothing that the boys can't handle. Nat is very experienced when it comes to supervising construction.'

Max remained silent for such a long time that Mia began to fidget.

'You're very knowledgeable on what's going on,' he murmured eventually.

And into that positive remark, Mia jumped feet-first.

If her job was at stake, what better way to secure it than to prove to him that she was worth what she was being paid?

'I was taken on to do the landscaping,' she explained with enthusiasm. 'As you know, the grounds are extensive! I should say that, in keeping with an eco-venture, I've made sure to clear as little of the indigenous plant life as possible. I'm a great believer in—'

'I'm getting the message here.' He paused.

Mia had hoped to sell her talents a little more comprehensively but she felt she had possibly done enough at least to sway him if he had been thinking about letting her go simply because she had refused to tell him where his sister was.

She wondered whether she should invite him to have a look at some of the ideas she had detailed in a series of scale drawings, show him how she intended to use some of the land for growing fruit and vegetables. Part of the work had already begun, as it was a big job and would have to be done in stages. She could walk him through it.

Then she thought about showing him around, talking it through with him, being in his presence yet again, and she decided to hold off for the moment.

At any rate, he certainly wasn't making any encouraging noises about her plans for his land. But he did continue to look at her in thoughtful silence until eventually she continued.

'I know it's a bit strange that I've become involved in more aspects of the hotel than you might have expected,' she grudgingly offered. When she tried to read what he was thinking, she drew a blank. It was disconcerting. 'It's a small team, really. If you exclude the…er…guys working on the building work, there's really only myself, Nat, Kahale and of course Izzy.'

'Who is no longer available…'

'But will be back here before you know it!' Mia said with a level of conviction she was far from feeling. Reading between the lines, Izzy had fled more than just a crap relationship and a broken heart. She'd also fled the confines of a life that had never allowed her to spread her wings and fly. She had done her utmost to let her creativity shine when it came to the hotel, to give herself that grounding, but she had hated the paperwork and dealing with people down the end of a phone line. Whenever possible, she had fobbed those jobs off on Mia, who had picked up the slack without complaint.

Yes, there was no question that Izzy would return and be better for it, but Mia wasn't going to bet on her optimistic prediction of 'within a week or so'…

'And in the meantime, you're here,' Max mused. 'And here is where we stand—I'm going to be stuck here, because I'm giving my sister the time she seems to need for reasons that are beyond me, but someone is going to have to step into her shoes and bring me up to date with what's been going on.' He looked at her, utterly relaxed and yet supremely forceful.

'What do you mean?' Mia knew exactly what he meant.

'I don't have Izzy, but you're here. Time to step up to the plate.'

CHAPTER THREE

THIS WAS A situation Max had not catered for. From the other side of the pond, things had seemed straightforward enough when he had boarded the plane to Honolulu. Irritating, but straightforward.

One wayward sister who had to be located and brought back to that little thing called *reality*—namely the job she had abandoned without prior warning. One friend who would spill the beans because she would find out fast enough that she had no choice. Quick debrief with Nat, probably with Izzy in tow so that she could be reminded in no uncertain terms of the very cushy number she was fortunate enough to have. And then he would be able to return to his high-powered life in the fast lane.

That was his comfort zone.

Max Stowe led a life that would have driven many to a nervous breakdown. He never stopped. Everything took second place to the demands of work. He knew that, accepted it and was indifferent when it came to changing his priorities. Why would he? He enjoyed control and he had ultimate control over every aspect of his life.

He worked hard. He liked the pressure. He had enough money to enjoy an expensive life a million times over, but that didn't mean he had any intention of ever slowing down. He worked long hours and, when he rested, he rested with women who knew the score, who knew that he was never going to be in it for the long term. He was a red-blooded male with a libido to match. He enjoyed the women he dated but he was intensely disciplined when it came to knowing just where they featured in his life. He'd never, not once, allowed his head to take second place to any other part of his body.

Buried deep in his formative years were lessons learnt about the havoc emotion caused and the disastrous roads it took people down. As the eldest in the family, he had registered, in ways neither James nor certainly Izzy ever had, the self-indulgence of his parents, who had been so absorbed in one another that parental responsibility was just a game they played at now and again.

He had been conveniently sent to boarding school at the age of seven. By the age of ten, he had given up on his parents showing any real interest in his achievements. By the time he'd hit adolescence, he'd stopped caring.

Bit by bit, he'd sealed the emotional side of himself off. He was naturally gifted academically, and could take his pick when it came to sport, so studying and sport became the two things he'd relied upon. You knew where you stood on a rugby pitch or in a physics exam. Once those values had been cemented, they had hardened over the years, and so here he was now. Pleased to be the controlling hand at the rudder, knowing exactly where his life was going and knowing that it was never going to deviate from the path he had carved out for himself.

Except…things at the moment weren't going quite according to plan, and that got on his nerves. He'd had no hesitation in rousing his PA at six that morning to brief her about various meetings that would have to be put on the back burner or delegated to a couple of his trusted CEOs. He had told her that James would be available should the need arise, but he was stretched dealing with his own arm of the family empire.

Now, sitting in the boardroom he had requisitioned from the hotel, waiting for Mia to show up, he tried to timetable his week going forward. Even dividing it into sound bites did little to paper over the fact that he really had no idea when he would be able to head back to London. The maximum amount of time he would spend here was a fortnight, but it was intensely frustrating not to be able to have a more precise idea of when within that two-week period his departure would take place.

He was sprawled back in the leather chair,

computer in front of him on the glossy marble conference table, staring out of the window at another dazzlingly sunny day, when the door opened quietly.

From behind it, Mia paused, heart hammering. He wasn't aware that she had pushed open the heavy boardroom door. He was absorbed in whatever he was thinking, which was probably work-related, given a laptop was open on the massive table in front of him.

She took a few seconds to look at his averted profile and the lazy sprawl of his muscular body as he gazed through the bank of floor-to-ceiling windows that looked out at a stunning vista of buildings and blue sky and, in the distance, the radiant blue-green ocean.

He was wearing a pair of faded jeans and a grey polo shirt and loafers. She wondered whether this was the most casual outfit ever to grace this fabulous space with its long walnut sideboard, on which someone had kindly placed plates filled with various breakfast pastries, its marble twenty-seater table and its elegant drapes.

Mostly, she wondered whether she should have knocked, but then she wasn't his secretary, although she did indeed work for him. She was filling in for Izzy. Bringing him up to date with stuff to do with the hotel. He probably would have this one meeting with her and that would be the end of their communications. He could pick Nat's brain for any additional information.

Couldn't he?

She had spent a restless night, head too full of the day's unexpected events to allow her much sleep.

Surprisingly, top of the agenda for things bothering her hadn't been the fact that he had shown up out of nowhere and tried to demand answers out of her, or the fact that she had released information about Izzy that had been said in confidence—even though at the time Izzy had said nothing about Mia keeping any of the information to herself.

No, what had bothered her, what had kept her awake, had been her own incomprehensible physical reaction to him. In her mind's eye, she had been able to envisage all too clearly for her liking the strong, chiselled lines of his lean, handsome face...the muscularity of his body...the sweep of those long, dark lashes...the brooding intensity of his eyes.

His appearance had impacted her in ways that were vaguely unsettling because they had come from nowhere and caught her unprepared.

She cleared her throat and he turned around. Thankfully, her legs did what she wanted them to do, and she walked towards him, not quite knowing where to sit at the enormous table. If she took the opposite end, she would need a megaphone to be heard.

He spared her the decision by almost imperceptibly nodding at the chair directly adjoining his and sitting up, waiting until she had shuffled into the seat.

He was casually dressed. She, on the other hand, had fished out the most formal outfit she could get her hands on. Her work uniform rarely strayed beyond the parameters of jeans or shorts and tee shirts, with the occasional sarong thrown in for when she was teaching surf to the kids at the weekend. She lived in flip flops, sandals or trainers.

Today she had opted for a sensible knee-length skirt and a blouse, neatly tucked into the waistband. And some proper shoes.

Was it her imagination or did she glimpse a flash of amusement in his eyes when he looked at her?

She pursed her lips and perched on the chair.

'Relax.'

'I've downloaded some facts and figures I thought you might want to have a look at.' Straight down to business. She reached into her backpack and extracted a plastic folder, which she held out to him. He ignored her outstretched hand, so she awkwardly dropped it onto the table.

'No need. I expect there's nothing there I haven't found out for myself.' He sat back, re-laxed, and looked at her for a few moments. 'First of all,' he drawled, compounding the image of a male utterly at ease by folding his hands behind his head, 'There's no need for you to change the way you dress because your role has slightly altered.'

Two hot patches of colour appeared on her cheeks. 'I don't think that a sarong, a baggy tee shirt and some flip-flops would be the right dress code for this sort of situation,' she said stiffly.

'Nor do you have to feel obliged to wear clothes you find uncomfortable,' Max returned gently.

Mia didn't say anything. He'd made very clear that she worked for him and she was going to have to curb the desire to snap back at everything he said.

'I spoke to Nat last night,' Max continued briskly. 'He brought me up to date with the supply shortages with the timber. What I'm getting is that Izzy may have been quite out of her depth. I thought I was doing her a favour in handing over more or less complete responsibility for guiding this project through from visual to completion. It seems I was mistaken.'

'She's only twenty-two!' Mia protested.

'You'd be surprised how capable a twenty-two-year-old can be when thrown into a situation,' Max replied coolly, his navy eyes guarded. 'We communicated by email, with the occasional phone call. I was under the impression that this was to be a top-of-the-range, no-expense-spared-when-it-came-to-luxury kind of hotel. From what Nat has said, that was far from what my sister envisaged.'

'I couldn't really comment on that,' Mia muttered.

'I'd planned on going through some of the financial figures with you here,' Max said crisply, shutting his laptop and standing, 'but I think I'd be better served if we leave immediately for the hotel so that I can see for myself exactly what the footprint on the ground looks like.'

He waited for her to get to her feet and then, heading towards the door, continued, 'We're going to be outside. We're going to be tramping through the foundations of the hotel. I don't suppose there will be any convenient air-conditioning so my suggestion would be for you to get out of those stiflingly hot clothes and wear what you would normally wear if you were working outside.'

Every word he said riled Mia. Not only had he managed to hijack her normal life but now, she having made a special effort to turn herself into someone resembling an assistant rather than the gardener she was, he saw nothing wrong in sending her off to get changed.

'Of course.' She stalked towards the door but before she could fling it open his hand was on her arm and she froze.

'I'll come with you to your house and wait for you.'

'Why?' Heart speeding up, she looked at him, banking down a flare of alarm.

'Because it makes sense. I have a driver. You can fill me in on the general design of the hotel on the way to your house and then he can deliver us to the hotel so that you can show me round.'

She nodded curtly and her lips were compressed as they headed down to the lobby and out into the blistering sun.

He was right. If she did anything outside in this weather, wearing these clothes, she would pass out.

But she still felt awkward as she slid into the back seat of the car and told his driver where she lived.

They were travelling in style. The driver was uniformed, with the stony expression of someone highly trained to conceal all emotion and only to speak when addressed. The car was a shiny, black top-of-the-range Mercedes with blacked-out windows and a level of air-conditioning that made her want to sigh with pleasure.

She stroked the soft leather with one finger and, when she glanced across to Max, it was to find that he was looking at her, a smile tugging the corners of his mouth.

'I can't help it,' Mia muttered defensively.

'Can't help what?'

'I don't think I've ever been in a car like this before,' she admitted. 'It's beyond luxurious.'

Max smiled, genuinely amused. He'd started the morning at precisely five a.m. He'd powered through a number of emails and spoken to whoever had been available at that hour, time differences taken into account. He had devoted a considerable amount of time to the situation with his sister, replaying in his head what Mia had told him—that Izzy had specifically requested he not contact her. *Specifically.* He had shrewdly noted Mia's discomfort when she had told him this and knew that Izzy's insistence on not wanting him to find her was probably even more urgent.

Mia would have tried to soften the harsh reality. That had hurt. He had been assiduous when it came to looking out for his sister and he couldn't deny that it hurt to realise that he had been found wanting.

It was something he had chosen to put out of his mind, however, because the main thing was the business of apprising himself of what had been happening in his absence. He had handed over too much responsibility to his sister, trusting that she would follow through.

At the back of his mind, he knew that he had made inaccurate assumptions and even more badly judged comparisons. Whilst he had taken on board the weight of premature responsibilities when his parents had died, when he himself had been the same age as his sister now, they were different people with different life experiences and different goals. Izzy wasn't him.

He had given her what he saw as a golden opportunity, and maybe it had been, but in all events it had been too soon for her.

She'd wanted to live her life on her terms. She hadn't wanted his interference then and she didn't want it now.

But introspection wasn't something he liked to indulge, and it had kick-started his day on a bad footing.

He'd hit the boardroom an hour and a half before Mia was due to show up, ample time to discover that conversations he had had with Izzy about the hotel and suggestions he had put her way because this was his third foray into the hotel business, albeit on a much, much smaller scale, had been largely ignored.

He'd taken his eye off the ball for the very first time when it came to work and he could have kicked himself.

Yet, when he had turned to see Mia framed in the doorway, all those feelings of edgy frustration had vanished.

He'd never seen anyone look so uncomfortable in his life before. She didn't want to be there, and she'd weirdly decided to wear a strange, starchy suit—which, her expression had managed to convey, was all his fault.

Yet even in the discomforting get-up, and even with her disgruntled, struggling-to-be-polite expression, she was still so stunningly pretty.

Then she'd sat down, he had breathed in the light scent of whatever flowery perfume she was wearing and he'd had to back away from proximity to her. Two hours breathing her in and seeing the tantalising flash of leg so close to his might stretch his powers of concentration a little too much.

At any rate, it made sense to go to the hotel with her so that she could talk him through the finer points. Yet here, in the confines of the car, there was a sizzling awareness of her that he couldn't seem to damp down.

'Rustic mosaic tiles,' he said flatly, angling his big body so that his back was against the car door and he could face her, legs sprawled apart. 'An absurd amount of wooden planks… Four-poster beds…'

'I beg your pardon?'

'I'm giving you a taster of some of the un-expected items I came across, and I've only just begun my search. Since you seem to know quite a bit about the hotel, care to tell me if any of these items make sense to you?'

His eyes drifted to her full lips. It irritated and bewildered him that he couldn't seem to focus when he was in her presence. Max knew that women behaved in a certain way when they were around him. Even the women he met on a business level. He was very much aware of the fact that they tailored their responses, aimed to please, strove to gain his attention.

He was used to that and he liked it. Life was pressured enough on the work front so, when it came to women, he liked things to be laid back and unchallenging.

Certainly, demanding women were a turn-off, so it was downright puzzling that he found himself so inexplicably drawn to the woman sitting next to him who had done nothing but bicker, argue and overreact from the very second he had announced who he was. Even before that, when he thought about it.

Hadn't her opening words to him been, *'Forget it'*?

She was looking at him narrowly, striving to remember that she was his employee, whilst no doubt wanting to launch into another diatribe.

She'd tied her hair back and he wanted to tell her that, however hard she'd tried to look businesslike, she had failed miserably because she was still as sexy as Hell.

He wondered what she would say, how she would react.

He wondered…what it would feel like to unbutton the prissy blouse she had chosen to wear and slip his hand underneath the bra, which he imagined would be a no-nonsense white affair. What would she look like half-naked? She had small breasts and he had a graphic image of his hand covering one of them, playing with her, watching her scowling, defensive face soften with passion.

A dark flush stained his sharp cheekbones. His imagination was running away and he would have to rein it in. Not simply because he didn't do loss of self-control but also because he didn't do mixing business with pleasure. Delectable she might be, but she worked for him, and as his employee she stood on the opposite side of a very well-defined divide.

Mia met his eyes steadily. He was scowling, his face dark, already prepared to jump the gun and lay into her because he had given Izzy orders—no doubt camouflaged as suggestions—and she had chosen to bypass them. His default position was attack mode, and she would have to be careful to remember that and not be lulled into any false sense of security if he happened to lay on his natural charm now and again.

She inhaled deeply, counted to ten and then said calmly, 'I do know some of the things Izzy had in mind for the hotel, as it happens, and I'm pretty sure you'll get on board once I run through them with you.'

Mia was not at all sure of any such thing. He was so...*rigid*—so very different from his sister. She had never met anyone as tightly controlled as him and she wondered if some of her fascination stemmed from that.

'This isn't my first venture into the hotel business,' Max informed her. He studied her from under the screen of sooty black lashes. 'I know what works.'

'What?' Mia asked a little breathlessly.

'Luxury. Unabashed luxury. People who

pay big money want a certain level of indulgence.'

'This is Hawaii…there's more scope to be casual here.'

'No matter if it's Timbuctoo,' Max said smoothly. 'You'd be surprised how much the wealthy tend to follow a certain pattern of behaviour.'

'You could be wrong.'

'When it comes to making money, I'm never wrong,' he said with a level of smooth self-assurance that was frankly mesmerising. 'When our parents died, I was catapulted fresh from university into the family business. I went from dissertations on mergers and productivity in commercial markets to having to work out how to put that into practice. I took the family business from where it was, comfortable but stagnating in the bottom percentile, and hauled it into the millennium. I learned, every step of the way, where to look for opportunities and how to make the most of them. I also learnt fast that it's not enough to have ideas or to put them into practice. It's even more important to know the beast you're dealing with.

'When it comes to hotels, people want to feel that they're being pampered, even if the pampering might be camouflaged. They don't want to pay a fortune, Mia, and find themselves swimming in a real lake, with very real algae and mud at the bottom. What they want is a sanitised pool pretending to be a lake so that they can feel as though they're in the middle of nature but without the tiresome, gritty lack of comfort.'

'That's so cynical.' Mia looked at his tough, handsome face and then found that she couldn't manage to tear her eyes away.

'If you want to get on in life—' Max shrugged '—you have to be cynical.'

Ten minutes later, Mia realised that they were pulling up outside her house.

She'd had no opportunity to talk about the hotel. She'd been sucked into frantic curiosity about his approach to life, had marvelled that he could be so world-weary when he was still in his mid-thirties. She'd found herself wondering how this all translated into his personal life and had blushed for ever letting her thoughts wander down that route.

If he hadn't taken a call, she was afraid that she might have asked him personal questions that were none of her business. Now it was a relief to hop out of the car and head inside the coolness of her house, with Max safely still on his call and barely seeming to notice that the car had stopped and that she had left it.

Her house was small with a wooden veranda at the back holding old wicker chairs and a bamboo table. It was her favourite spot to relax because her back garden, which was a mixture of earth and patchy grass, overlooked the sea, albeit the view was a distant one. She barely paused to gaze out at that view now, instead heading directly to her bedroom. Now that she was out of the air-conditioned confines of the Mercedes, she couldn't wait to get out of the skirt and blouse, and she rid herself of both in record time.

She'd put a lot of thought into what she had chosen to wear to meet Max and, uncomfortable as it had been, the outfit had conferred some essential distance between them.

She would have to wear comfortable clothes to show him around the hotel, which was currently a building site, so she dressed accordingly in jeans, a tee shirt and her walking boots.

He was still on his call when she slipped back into the car a mere fifteen minutes after it had arrived at her house.

She was still clutching the backpack and now she extracted the sheaf of papers she had taken with her to the boardroom and which he had casually dismissed.

'Ah.' Max ended his phone call and shoved the mobile phone into his trouser pocket. 'You decided to dump the office garb. Good. Feel a little less restricted?'

'I didn't feel *restricted*,' Mia rebutted. 'But this is more appropriate for looking around a building site.'

'Which is going to be a more condensed visit, as it happens. I'll have a quick look round, but I've scheduled a meeting with

Nat for this afternoon to discuss various aspects of the costings that will have to be assessed before anything further gets ordered. If I don't like the direction all of this is going, then everything gets halted, and I'll make sure what I want is followed to the last letter.'

'And what about when Izzy returns? She's put her heart and soul into her plans for the hotel. I know they're probably not what you had in mind, but she's spent a lot of time coming up with ideas...'

'That was then and this is now,' Max imparted flatly. 'I can't hang around waiting for my sister to decide that she's got her act together and is ready to return, and even if she does...' He paused for a few seconds, then raked his fingers through his hair. 'Then her role may need to be revisited.'

'What do you mean?'

'If there are aspects of the job she doesn't like, then there's no point to forcing her to do them.' He wearily pressed his fingers over his eyes but, when he looked at her, he was once more in complete control. 'I intend to hire a full-time accountant to deal with the day-to-day financial running of the place and in time, when things start gathering momentum, I will ensure a team is taken on.'

In that moment, Mia felt all her prejudices against him slip and slide uneasily beneath her feet.

When it came to his sister, it was clear that underneath the hard, dictatorial exterior was a real well of love. He might have been too aggressive when it had come to directing her life, but it hadn't been for a lack of strong, fraternal protectiveness.

Life experiences changed people, made them veer off in all sorts of directions that sometimes made no sense to the people around them.

Wasn't she a victim of that herself?

She had married young in a subconscious desire to repeat what her parents had done, what her siblings had done. Marrying young, having a family and replicating what she knew had been a given when she and Kai had married. They had both gone into marriage blithely assuming a happy-ever-after ending, blithely assuming that they would slide seamlessly into the noisy, wonderful chaos of family life.

It had unravelled with speed. The easy familiarity they had always shared had very quickly become the tension of two very young people who had never had to put their relationship to the test. The business of sharing space had revealed flaws they had never noticed before.

But divorce had come at a price. She had retreated from the business of finding love and had made her checklist of required traits so meticulous that the years had gone by. With each passing year, Mia had known that her ability to *feel* was shrinking just a little bit more.

So who was she to point fingers at Max? He was as cold as ice, but having responsibility for two siblings when you were barely out of your teens yourself would have been punishing.

'That's probably a good idea,' she agreed.

'Any interest in applying for the job?'

Mia relaxed and laughed. 'No chance. As it happens, I'm pretty good with the books, but I like the outdoor life.'

'Change of plan.'

'Sorry?'

'You can sit in on my meeting with Nat. He's the supervisor on the job and he will have a pretty good idea of the supply chain, because I know he's been dealing with some of them, but if you're good at accounts then your contribution might be useful.'

'I'm not dressed for a meeting in that boardroom!'

She stared down at the casual clothes and then blushed as their eyes met and held.

Her bra was the thinnest of cotton, just a sliver of stretchy fabric. She felt the push of her nipples as they swelled and tightened under his leisurely appraisal. She was hot all over, her skin tingling. She followed the trajectory of his gaze when she licked her upper lip as it rested for a crazily long time on the innocent gesture.

She'd thought that her divorce had put her into a deep freeze but, if that was the case, she was certainly thawing out now, big time, and had been since she had first clapped eyes on him.

She whipped her gaze away but her breathing was laboured and her fingers were linked so tightly together that when she stared down she could see the pale brown of the stretched skin of her knuckles.

'I wouldn't worry about whether you're over-dressed or under-dressed when you're with me,' Max murmured lazily. 'You could wear a bin bag at a Michelin-starred restaurant and no one would dare raise an eyebrow.'

He paused for so long that eventually she got up the courage to look at him, while her heart thumped like a runaway train inside her.

'At any rate,' he added, dropping his eyes and shifting his big body in the seat next to her, 'you look pretty damn good whatever you decide to wear.'

CHAPTER FOUR

HAVING ONLY EVER worked for herself since she had left college, it was something of a shock to the system to discover that working for Max involved jumping at his command and keeping pace with the speed of his intellect as he went through every detail of the hotel, from the amount of nails ordered, to the teams on standby for when the bulk of the work was to begin.

Their scheduled trip to see the hotel had been put on hold but she knew that he had gone there briefly with Nat the day before. It was the first time in the four days since he had commandeered her life that she had busied herself on a couple of the other small projects she'd had in the mix which required face-to-face meetings and brief land surveys.

Not that she worked with him every minute of the day. He worked in the boardroom, which he seemed to have appropriated for his needs and his alone, and much of the time he was involved in all sorts of conference calls to who knew how many people scattered across the globe. But, when it came to the hotel, he expected her to be at hand, ready to answer any questions he had.

He'd had no problem in telling her that whatever other jobs she had would have to be put on ice, because time was money, and he didn't have a lot of time to sort out the unfinished business his sister had left behind.

'But,' she had told him on day one, 'my job at the hotel has to be taken a step at a time. I've done all the drawings and plans for what I would like to do with the surrounding land, but actual purchasing and planting will have to be done in stages, and can't reasonably begin until work on certain parts of the hotel are underway.'

'And?' Max had quirked a questioning eyebrow. He had been sitting in front of his computer, a commanding presence at the long table in the boardroom, his body language telling her that he wasn't expecting a long-winded conversation with her, because he had things to do, so could she make it brief.

Standing to one side, she was awkwardly conscious of her crisp, clean clothes that were somewhere between the prissy starched out-fit she had worn that very first time she had gone to see him, and the outdoor gear she spent most of her days in. Neat shoes, a pair of grey cotton mid-calf trousers and a tee shirt tidily tucked into the waistband of the trousers.

'And in my spare time I focus on a few other jobs. None of them are particularly big but I need all the work I can get.'

'Why?'

'Sorry?'

'You're generously paid by me.'

'Yes, I know that, but in this line of work it's not just about the money. This job will finish in under a year and I need to have other things in the pot that I can turn to. I give one hundred and ten percent when it comes to the hotel and that includes all the extra duties I've taken on over the past few months...'

'Okay, spare me the highlights and lowlights. You're not auditioning for a job. Fact is, I won't be setting aside dedicated time for hotel business. I have a lot of other deals going on, deals that I should be handling back in London, but which I now have to handle here because Izzy's done a runner.'

He had let that settle into the silence between them, a reminder that he was there because he had chosen to give his sister the benefit of the doubt and leave her be until she sorted herself out. A reminder that he had *chosen* to listen to what she, Mia, had advised rather than following his natural instinct to bypass her when he hadn't got what he had come for and hire someone to locate his sister.

'What are these other jobs?' he had demanded.

'I have some tenders I'm looking at...ideas I need to commit to paper. A couple of meetings lined up as well...'

'In which case…' he had gestured magnanimously at the boardroom table '…you can sit anywhere you like at this table and do whatever you have to do right here. That way, you're at hand when I need to ask you a question. As for meetings? You have my word that after five your time is yours.'

He wasn't about to give way on this because he was the sort of man who never gave way on anything.

Mia had thus discovered the joys of the very type of office job she had often teasingly reminded her sisters was the very depths of boring.

The puzzle for her was that she enjoyed it more than she had thought she would, more than she thought she *should.*

She perched opposite him. She'd brought all her work with her and she had to admit that the surroundings were pretty fabulous. Pastries and coffee were on tap. It was beautifully air-conditioned and, in fairness, he had a capacity to focus that was incredible. When he became involved in conference calls, when he sat frowning in front of his computer, scrolling and making notes, when he spoke to CEOs, voice clipped and every word succinct and to the point, she knew that she ceased to exist.

And when she was in that place where she ceased to exist...her eyes strayed. She couldn't help it. She sneaked glances at him, committing to memory the way he sat with his chair swivelled at an angle...the way he stared off into the distance when he was concentrating...the way he absently tapped his pen on the table when he was working on his computer, a gesture that summed up the restless energy of his personality.

Today, they were going to be meeting with Nat at the hotel, but Mia was already running late.

As luck would have it, and for the first time in weeks, dazzling blue skies had been replaced with driving rain.

It was a little after four and Mia had cycled from one of her clients, a guy with a roof garden and ambitious plans to turn it into a vegetable paradise with wild flowers in tubs. She had had to gently dissuade him from plans to add a couple of bee hives to the mix because he liked honey.

The sun had been shining when she'd left her house but in the space of a couple of hours the skies had gone from cerulean blue to leaden grey and then the heavens had opened.

Instead of the twenty-minute ride to the hotel, she had taken over forty-five minutes, and it was after five by the time she pulled away from the main drag and along the quiet side roads that led to the construction site.

The hotel was located in a brilliant spot, a taxi ride from the city but edging towards the sea, against a backdrop of stunning land dense with trees and threaded with water-falls.

It was the perfect getaway, a child-free hotel where there would be no limits to the luxury on offer.

The site had been very carefully chosen and it was a brilliant example of the magical juxtaposition on the island of wild nature, urban seaside and captivating metropolis.

The sun was fading by the time she skidded to a stop and wiped the rain from her eyes to look at what had been accomplished over the past few months.

Less than Max had expected. She knew that from a couple of the things he had said after his abbreviated visit there with Nat. In fairness, she couldn't blame him. The schedule had been pushed back several times because first of all Izzy had decided not to go with any of the suggestions her brother had made and then, having charted a different route, she had dithered when it had come to making her mind up on several crucial points.

Tarpaulin protected some of the half-built rooms, and for the rest foundations had been laid and were patiently awaiting stage two. The weeds coiling round the cement and bricks seemed to indicate that several of those foundations had given up all hope of being completed and were happy to wave a white flag and kick back for the duration.

Mia leapt off the bike while shoving it upright all in one smooth motion and sprinted towards the one bit of the hotel that was the least forlorn.

The extensive kitchen was pretty much done, which was to say that there were walls, a roof, concrete ground and various partitions, gaps and openings where appliances would eventually fit. The space was enormous. She arrived in a soaking rush to find Max already there and waiting for her.

The construction workers had kitted out the place as best they could so that they could do some very rudimentary cooking. There was a kettle, some mugs, an electric hot plate and a motley assortment of mismatched chairs.

A working mini-fridge was plugged into a socket and there was an electric fan.

'You're late.'

Still trying to dry herself the best she could in the absence of a towel, Mia screeched to a halt and glared at him.

He was as dry as a bone and had helped himself to a mug of coffee, which he was loosely holding, half-resting it on his lap. He dwarfed the chair, his long legs stretched out in front of him and crossed at the ankles. He looked dry and comfortable and utterly elegant in an understated way. Faded jeans, tan loafers and a white short-sleeved tee shirt.

'Thank you for pointing that out,' Mia snapped. She gave a final squeeze of her hair and saw that he was holding out a handkerchief for her. Pride made her want to ignore it completely, but pride would have to take second place to practicality, and right now she just wanted some part of her to be dry.

She wiped her face and handed him back the handkerchief. It was late, so a completely wasted trip, because there was no way she would be able to show him anything now.

She'd cycled like a maniac to get here and his opening words were *you're late*?

Mia thought he was lucky she didn't hurl something at him, and she wouldn't have cared whether she was a handsomely paid employee or not.

'I cycled here,' she said through gritted

teeth. 'It was fine when I left but, since I'm not a meteorologist, I didn't predict this thunderstorm, so it took a lot longer than I'd banked on.'

Max stood up and continued to look at her while she cast him a glowering, baleful, sullen look.

'You're soaked.'

'Thanks for pointing out the obvious.'

'You should have pulled over and phoned me to cancel. It wouldn't have been the end of the world.'

Mia didn't say anything because that hadn't even occurred to her. She'd been running on adrenaline, not paying as much attention as she should to her client, keen to head off, because the thought of seeing Max had been a hot, driving excitement in her veins.

So hot and so driving that common sense had taken a back seat. Of course she should have called him! As soon as the clouds had started turning an angry black, she should have pulled over, got out her mobile phone and explained the situation. An idiot would have been able to figure out that driving rain would make a nonsense of her timings.

'Come on.' He urged her towards the door, hand cupping her elbow. 'There's a half-dirty tea towel hanging around here somewhere, but no convenient pile of towels, I'm afraid. I'll get you home.'

'Get me home?'

'Nothing to do here. Way too rainy, way too late and way too dark. My driver is waiting.'

She was being shuffled out of the place, barely concentrating on what she was doing or where they were going.

'My bike…'

'Will live to ride another day. Now, run!'

She obeyed instinctively. She was already so wet. The thought of getting any wetter didn't bear thinking about. She was cold too, her teeth chattering and her clothes clinging to her like cling film.

She literally bolted for the dry sanctuary of the car, and she would have made it as well if the wretched, soggy, uneven ground of a building site hadn't conspired to bring her crashing to her knees.

She was racing one minute, and the next she was lying in a heap on the ground, and when she hurriedly began to prop herself back up her foot buckled under her and she gave a yelp of pain.

The rain washed over her, sharply pricking her skin, and overhead there was a crack of thunder that made her start.

All of this took place in a matter of seconds—the running, the falling, the roar of thunder and then the horrifying realisation that he was sweeping her off her feet and sprinting to the car. His driver had opened an umbrella, the passenger door was open, then they were both inside the car and the door was slammed shut behind them.

'Your foot,' Max said as the car purred away from the site and back out towards the city. 'How much does it hurt?'

'It'll be fine,' Mia muttered.

'There's nothing to be gained by being a martyr. Do I need to take you to hospital?

Only you can tell me exactly how bad it is, so don't lie.'

'It's fine.' She tentatively tried to circle her ankle and winced.

'Right. We'll go back to your house and I'll have a look but, if I'm in any doubt, I'm getting a doctor out.'

'Don't be ridiculous!'

'I'm not being ridiculous, Mia,' he said coolly. 'All precautions will be taken, because the last thing I need is a lawsuit for negligence. So if I think a doctor needs to come out, then out he comes, whether you agree or not.'

'You think I'd *what*?' Mia gaped, momentarily distracted from the pain in her ankle and the way her clothes were becoming glued to her body. 'Sue you because I was an idiot who fell over?'

Max shrugged. 'As it happens, I don't, but who knows?'

'God, what sort of world do you live in?'

'What do you mean by that?'

'Well, it seems that in *your* world women

are either open to a bit of blackmail or else trying to sue you for something that's not your fault! In other words, you're not exactly prepared to give women the benefit of the doubt, are you?'

She looked at him narrowly and was perversely satisfied at the dark flush of colour that delineated his razor-sharp cheekbones. For once, she'd caught him on the back foot, and it felt great.

He looked away, and she wanted to prod at the sore spot she had found, because he *got* to her and it felt good that she could likewise get to him.

'When you get to the top of the ladder,' he said, turning to her, his voice matter-of-fact, borderline indifferent, 'it pays to put *trust* at the back of the queue.'

'You don't trust *anyone*?' Mia asked with disbelief. She might have gone through the misery of a divorce, and she may have built her own ivory tower to protect herself from getting hurt again, but that didn't mean she didn't *trust* people.

Her family...her friends... Her default position wasn't that she had to be on red-hot alert one hundred percent of the time because everyone was capable of hiding a knife behind their back.

She felt a wave of compassion. He might be as hard as granite, but you didn't get to a position of such cynicism without your past experiences putting you there.

'I feel sorry for you, Max,' she said quietly, and his eyebrows shot up.

'Should I be touched or irritated?'

'I expect you'll be irritated,' she confirmed. 'You said that I'm on the lookout for an argument all the time. Well, I'm no different to you, am I? I'm just being honest. It must be a lonely life if you can't trust anyone at all. You might have all the money in the world but if you're alone in your glass tower then what's the point?'

'I cope.'

Two words signalling the end of the conversation. He didn't look irritated. He looked bored.

A door had been slammed in her face, and she couldn't blame him, because commenting on his private life was way out of order.

He was her boss and her role was to liaise with him about the hotel, end of story. Her role was not to make wise proclamations about his life choices. She wasn't a landscape gardener turned shrink!

Her cheeks stung and she looked away, and with relief realised that they were nearing her house. She'd barely noticed the journey. She'd barely noticed her soaked clothes or her foot!

The driver was out of the car as soon as he'd killed the engine, umbrella at the ready. Max moved with similar alacrity, removing all chance of her taking a stand and trying to hobble to the door unaided.

In fact, her feet weren't allowed to touch the ground at all. Swept off her feet twice in a day, Mia thought with a touch of mild hysteria, and not in the way she'd ever imagined it happening.

'It's in the front pocket,' she muttered, before he could ask her where the house key was, and he duly located it and pushed open the door.

'I'll call you when I'm ready,' he said to the driver, who nodded and returned to the car.

The rain followed them through the open door, but then Max slammed it shut, and it became a steady, noisy beating against the roof and walls.

This was not how he had imagined the day panning out. Of course, it was essential that he had a walk through with her. Not only was she knowledgeable when it came to the accounts system but her main job involved the outside space, the land, and he needed to have an idea of how she intended to utilise the space. When he had discussed the hotel with his sister well over a year ago when it had been in the embryonic stage, he had suggested an infinity pool and all the various outdoor luxuries that came with that, including a state-of-the-art bar nestled among the trees where cocktails and drinks could be served on a more or less non-stop basis.

All those ideas had gone down the drain, so

it was necessary to know exactly what was destined to replace it, because the financial projections were all over the place.

Yes, this was a necessary trip, but even so he had been studiously putting it off.

Just having her sit at the other end of that boardroom table had been a challenge.

He'd been *aware* of her in ways that made a joke of his legendary self-control. He'd had to conduct most of his conversations on the phone, with his chair angled in such a way that she was just on the periphery of his vision, because every time he'd looked at her—her, head downbent, chin propped in the palm of her hand, her brown hair falling to one side—he'd had to fight against getting a hard-on.

It was crazy, and he didn't like himself for it, but he hadn't been able to do a thing about it. If he could have shouted questions across the table, he would have, but she'd had to edge next to him to stare at the same facts and figures on the same computer and her proximity had been great at messing with his head.

He wanted her. That was what it came down to. She was off-limits, but he wanted her, and the more he tried to ignore the tug at his senses the harder the tug was.

So he had deferred the inevitable trip to the hotel, and he certainly hadn't envisaged a sudden torrential downpour bringing him to this place, in her house, with her in his arms.

She was as light as a feather. He could have lifted her with one hand. And was she aware that the way those wet clothes clung...?

He'd fought to stop himself from staring. He knew that he'd reacted somewhat more aggressively than the occasion demanded when she had fallen and done whatever she'd done to her foot.

Had he really said something about getting a doctor because he had to protect himself against a possible lawsuit?

He had opened the door wide to her comments about the way he lived his life. Not her business, and he could definitely care less, but she had got under his skin and he wasn't sure whether that was because he was just so hyper-aware of her or because she insisted on ignoring all the *Do Not Trespass* signs everyone else managed to read very clearly.

She got to him in every way, and now here he was. In her house.

He looked around him and headed in the direction of the bedroom, while she remained passive in his arms, clearly having given up on fighting him. He could feel her warmth radiating beyond the wet clothes, the softness of her legs and the slightness of her body.

She was so *natural*—so lacking in any artifice. There was no make-up for the rain to wash away.

Never had he been more aware of his body or more alert to the temptation to hold her close, keep holding her, kiss her, touch her...

'You need to change,' he said abruptly.

He looked around him at her small house, with lots of wood and a feeling of homeliness. He'd glanced at the kitchen as he'd walked past and had seen colourful cupboards and an old pine table. The furniture in the living room was squashy and mismatched and the overhead fan was desultory. Here, in the bedroom, the double bed was covered with some kind of old-fashioned patchwork quilt, and there was a rocking chair by the window that overlooked a very pretty, panoramic view of shrubs and flowers and, in the distance, sand leading down to the sea.

The rain continued to pelt against the windows. If it hadn't been raining, and if night hadn't begun creeping in, casting long, dark shadows, Max was pretty sure he would have been able to hear the roll of the sea through the windows and see a blaze of stars in the sky.

Never one to get swept up in appreciating the scenery, he was momentarily disconcerted. He looked round to see her rising to her feet and he shook his head.

'Tell me where to look and I'll get what you want.'

Judging from her stubborn expression, he was guessing that the last thing she wanted was to direct him to her drawers so that he could fish out dry clothes for her, but she did as she was asked.

'Need help putting these clothes on?' He looked at her. 'It's going to be tricky getting out of those wet things.'

'I can manage.'

'Well, if you find you can't, then I'm within shouting distance. In fact, I'll wait right outside the door. Call me when you're dressed. I'm going to inspect your ankle, and don't even attempt to hobble out to me.'

Mia muttered something under her breath and looked at him with sulky hostility. 'You mean just in case I topple over and sue you for personal injury?'

Max shot her an impatient look and raked his fingers through his hair.

'Okay. I apologise for that.'

Their eyes tangled and her breathing picked up. She nodded and he hesitated fractionally.

'I've learnt that the only person I can trust is myself,' he told her heavily. 'It's just the way I'm built.'

Mia nodded and some of the hostility

drained away. What did he mean by that? No one was *built* to be distrustful. She waited until he had left the bedroom and shut the door behind him.

She was as exhausted, as if she'd run a marathon, by the time she had changed into the loose-fitting cotton bottoms, baggy tee shirt and fresh underwear.

The torrential rain had subsided to a steady drumbeat, but she still had to shout to be heard, and she was as tense as a bowstring when he pushed open the door, glass of water in one hand and in the other a couple of painkillers that he held out to her.

'These might take the edge off. Found them in one of your kitchen cupboards.'

Mia silently accepted the proffered tablets and automatically flinched as he levered himself down until he was kneeling at her feet like a supplicant as she sat on the edge of the bed. Or a guy about to propose to the woman of his dreams. A fine film of perspiration beaded her upper lip.

'I'm going to just try and feel my way around your ankle.' He looked up at her.

Mia was finding it very hard to actually hear a word he was saying because she was so conscious of his fingers on her skin, gently, very gently, stroking her tender, sensitive ankle. She was captivated by his eyes. Her breathing slowed and her mouth went dry. She felt giddy.

'I guess you're wondering why I should know anything about ankles and sprains,' he offered, and she nodded mutely. 'Well, believe it or not,' he continued, in the same soothing, best bedside manner voice as he began manipulating her foot in tiny, barely discernible circles, 'I did a summer job at a hospital when I was eighteen.'

'You did? Ouch, that *hurts*.'

'I'm sorry. It's going to a bit, I'm afraid. Try not to think about it.' He looked up and smiled crookedly. 'Think about me instead.'

'About you...' She did as he asked and then blinked a little unsteadily. Not a good command to give, because now all she could think about was his hands moving up from her ankle, up along her calf, slipping under the baggy bottoms to slide over her inner thigh...to go further...

Heat rushed through her body.

'Think about me working at a hospital. I was no more than a dogsbody, but you'd be amazed at what a dogsbody can pick up, and I've always been very good when it comes to picking things up.'

His voice was so quiet and so calming that she was aware of the pain in her ankle, whilst almost *not* being aware of it. He was very thorough and strangely tender for someone so big.

He told her about his hospital job. She really wasn't sure whether he was making it all up to distract her or whether he actually *had* worked in a hospital for three months.

He certainly seemed to know what he was doing.

When he asked her to tell him about her family, she sighed and complied. He vanished for a couple of minutes and returned with the first aid box she kept in the bathroom.

He was distracting her. She knew that. He wasn't interested in hearing about her family. Why would he be? She'd spent the past few days sitting opposite him and he'd barely noticed her existence, except on those occasions when he'd looked up and engaged her in something about the hotel. Other than that, she could have been a pot plant on the sideboard next to the platters of breads and pastries.

So did he really want to hear about her sprawling family? Her sisters? Her nieces and nephews? Or about that time when she was eight and they'd all gone on a family picnic by the sea, and she'd wandered off and ended up spending the night in the forest because they hadn't been able to find her for love nor money? Was he really as interested as he appeared to be when she told him about school, and about wanting to be different from her sisters, wanting to avoid university and an office job?

He seemed to be, because he kept asking questions, while busying himself with the bandage, wrapping it around her now swollen ankle with painstaking care.

He was a persuasive listener. The tablets had kicked in and the throbbing in her ankle had eased. The tension had seeped out of her and she'd never felt so relaxed.

Relaxed enough to sigh as she considered all the stuff she'd been through… Relaxed enough to say, as he neatly began finishing the job he had begun with the bandage, 'I guess it's because I come from such a close family that I ended up getting married so young…'

CHAPTER FIVE

'*MARRIED?*'

It wasn't often that Max was shocked, but he was shocked to the core now.

He almost burst out laughing at himself and his erroneous assumptions. Was his version of a divorced woman so one-dimensional? Did he really think that all divorcees were hard, bitter and plastered with war paint?

No. He didn't. But it was a telling assumption, and for the first time he found himself a little unsettled at realising just how pervasive his cynicism had become over the years. It coloured all his opinions and every aspect of his life.

Mia had told him that she felt sorry for him. Naturally, that was a laughable criticism. Anyone sharp enough to have mechanisms in place to deflect the slings and arrows of uncertain fate could never be an object of pity. The thought of it was ridiculous.

And yet, when he thought about it, his life was so intensely controlled...

He was accustomed to obedience on the work front. He might have groped his way for a while, when he had been thrust into a position of responsibility at the age of twenty-two. He had been surrounded by men and women twice his age. Many of them he had been forced to let go. Many more he had been forced to relocate. He had gritted his teeth and done what he had had to do. Life in a boarding school from the age of seven had toughened him. Sacking people to refine a business that would have to pay for his siblings had toughened him even further.

And now, many years later and with a business that was a thousand times bigger, he had learnt every aspect of control.

Handing over the building and running of this hotel to Izzy was the first time he had ever let go of the reins and look where it had got him.

He should have been the overlord in the equation, and everything would have run to plan. He would have had his hotel with its marble and glass and infinity pool and wouldn't now be wading through a bunch of designs, purchases and supply chains that shouldn't have been required in the first place.

The truth was, though, that his control extended way beyond what happened in his sprawling empire. When it came to women, he allowed no one past a certain point. He had been raised with the consequences of impulse. His parents had specialised in that to the exclusion of everything else. He had been brought up to distrust the so-called power of love and the irrational need to let other people in. His parents had certainly been indulgent when it had come to their all-consuming love, and in the process had ignored everything and everyone else, including their kids. Or at least *him.*

Holding the world at a distance had been one of his strengths. But now he wondered just how insular he had made his fabulous, moneyed world. He let no one in. He knew his parameters at all times.

Coming here had been a step out of his intensely controlled comfort zone. Under normal circumstances, were one of his smaller projects to need a helping hand on the ground, he would dispatch a member of staff. But he had needed to find his sister, so he'd made the trip himself.

And, since then, where was all that control he had always held dear?

He had arrived to find his ideas for the hotel in tatters. His aim to find his sister and leave within a couple of days had been trashed. He seemed to be permanently engaged in a standoff with a woman he couldn't go near without wanting to touch.

There was a battle raging inside him.

Sure, he was attracted to her. She was an incredibly attractive woman.

He'd been out with very many incredibly attractive women. So why was it that this particular one had managed to get under his skin in a way no other woman had?

It made no sense because, beyond the physical appeal, she should have been a turn-off.

She'd kicked off by not telling him where Izzy was. That in itself should have solved the problem of hanging around. He should have just gone ahead and taken the practical route of hiring someone to find her. It would have been easy. Not the most desirable option, but an easy one, given the fact that Mia had dug her heels in and refused to co-operate. Hire someone to do the job, get Izzy back at the hotel within hours—job done, bye-bye Hawaii and hello to the concrete jungle that was the city of London.

But he hadn't.

He'd listened to her—but had that put paid to her mouthiness? Not in the least. She felt utterly free, it seemed, to say exactly what was in her mind. Sometimes, he could tell that she was trying hard to hold back, despite the fact that she worked for him, but the thread that held her back from speaking her mind was gossamer-thin and often broke.

And yet, bewilderingly, he didn't seem to object as much as he knew he should. He was beginning to think that, the more she tried his patience, the more attracted he was to her and the faster his self-discipline got flushed down the pan.

He was her employer! She worked for him. He had always made a point of keeping business very far removed from pleasure. You let someone who worked for you into your life, and you lost control of the reins. That had always been his motto.

And yet, not even her status could detract from her appeal.

And now, finding out that she'd been married…

Been married? Or still was…?

Had she been clear?

'Where is he now?' Max asked abruptly. He stood up and stretched his joints, then cast a satisfied look at the job he had done bandaging her foot. 'And don't try to stand. It looks like a nasty sprain. Bit of swelling but I suspect a day or so of painkillers and keeping it off the ground will do the trick.' He looked at her. She was rain-washed. Her hair was drying in a spiky way but it did nothing to detract from her sexiness.

'So?' Never one to dig deep when it came to women's backstories, he now found that he was burning with curiosity and impatient to continue the conversation.

'So what? I won't stand on the foot. At least not right at the moment. And thank you for… you know…bandaging this up. You didn't have to.'

'The guy you married. Where is he now?'

'Oh. Kai.'

'That his name?' He was still getting his head round the fact that the woman now resting her bandaged foot on the stool he had brought for her, the woman with the sparkling brown eyes and skin as soft as silk, could have been married…could still be, for that matter.

'He lives in Honolulu with his new wife, as it happens.'

'You're incredibly sanguine about that.'

'You think I should be bitter?'

'I think it would be understandable.' He pulled a chair closer to her and dropped down into it. What did the guy look like? More to the point, what had gone wrong? Curiosity dug deep.

'I was very young. We both were. We knew each other from school. You could say that we mixed in the same crowd and then, at some point, we became an item. Both of us came from large families and after we left college it just seemed natural for us to...take things to the next level.'

'You drifted into marriage.'

'Sounds awful, but we had really high hopes. In fact...' She paused and sharply looked away. 'It never occurred to us that it would all fall apart at the seams. That's how cocky and confident we were. But as it turned out we were way too young and, much as we got along, we'd never shared space together.

We did everything as part of a group most of the time. We surfed and went to parties and hung out. We liked each other and we translated that into something else.'

'And then...?'

'You don't have to pretend to be interested in my life, Max,' she said gently. 'And you don't have to feel that you need to hang around here for a bit longer because you've been kind enough to bandage my foot.'

'I seldom do anything because I feel pressured,' he returned drily. 'Tell me what happened. I'm interested.'

'Things went wrong.' She shrugged. 'We started arguing. Kai wasn't cut out for staying in. He still wanted to party all the time. We thought we'd be great but in the end we couldn't even play house. It all started unravelling and eventually we called it a day.'

'And yet you seem to have gone past that pretty successfully.'

'I learnt from it.' Mia tilted her chin and firmed her mouth. 'That was years ago, and I made my mind up after that that I would never jump into anything without really testing the waters first. I'd have to be sure that any guy I went out with was the right one.'

Max wanted to laugh. Was there such a thing as 'the right one'? He very much doubted it. There were the loved-up and oblivious, like his parents. That seldom lasted. The magic wore off and in the blink of an eye someone was getting up to something they shouldn't with someone else. Too much fairy dust never augured well for the institution of marriage. Boredom had a nasty way of setting in and *then* where was the fairy dust? On the ground, being swept up by a disillusioned spouse.

Of course, in the case of his parents, the overpowering 'I only have eyes for you' love had lasted, but to the detriment of the kids they'd had.

Whichever way you looked at it, handing your emotions over to someone else and asking them to return the favour was never a good idea.

The 'right one' didn't exist.

A life lived logically was a good life, he mused. And if he ever decided to get married, well, a logical union would be just the ticket. Something that made sense. A business proposition, in a manner of speaking.

His eyes met hers and he held her gaze until she blushed and eventually looked away.

That blush said a lot, he thought with lazy satisfaction. He'd noticed it before—the way she slid her eyes away if he looked at her for too long, and the way she focused on him when she figured he wasn't looking.

A Pandora's box begging to be opened and he clenched his jaw, trying hard to stifle temptation at its source.

'You must be hungry,' he growled. 'I am.' He stood up and strolled without his usual grace to the window that gave out onto a dark, rainy and windswept night.

'I… There's no need…'

Max, still struggling to hang on to his self-control after too much introspection, and way too much interest in a woman who should be no more than another employee, was more brusque than intended when he replied. 'Repeat—I don't do anything because I feel obliged to. Tell me what you want to eat.'

'I could make something.'

'Italian food? French food? Chinese food? Name it.'

'But Max…'

He'd flipped his phone out and gave her an enquiring, impatient look.

'Okay…anything. Chinese food.'

It took him under five minutes to instruct his dedicated driver to fetch the food as soon as possible. The conversation was brief. He simply told the guy to put a call in to the restaurant with the best Chinese cuisine in the city, give his name and ask them to bring enough to feed two generously.

It never failed to impress Mia just how much money talked. She knew the restaurant the driver would order the food from and they didn't do take away. But he would get one without any trouble because he was obscenely rich. Rich enough to buy the restaurant. Rich enough to have the luxury of never doing anything he didn't want to do because he felt compelled.

The air he breathed and the world he lived in were far removed from hers. He'd arranged that they meet at his partly-built hotel so that she could walk him through some of Izzy's ideas. Instead, here he was in her home, bandaging her ankle, and she wondered if he resented the call on his time.

'I'm sorry...' she began awkwardly.

He had returned to his original position on one of the wide, squashy chairs and now he tilted his head to one side and looked at her questioningly.

'Are you going to apologise for my being here?' he asked drily. 'Because, if you are, then it will turn out to be a replay of the conversation where you tell me that I didn't have to, and I can't be bothered to repeat my response to you.'

'You might have had plans for the evening,' she mumbled.

'My plans were to work.'

'You must miss your...er...life in England.'

Somehow he'd ended up knowing a great deal about her and she wanted to find out something about *him*. Was that so unusual? Here they were, and the circumstances had shifted the normal barrier between them. She felt less like his employee and more like just another person.

Besides, they had to talk about *something*. It would be a disaster if they just sat and stared at one another in agonising silence, while her vivid imagination had a laugh at the expense of her common sense.

She hadn't been with a guy on her own for a long time.

The handful of dates she'd been on had been conducted with the buzz of anonymous chaperones all around, people coming and going on the beach, or in a bar or in a busy restaurant.

A sense of intimacy feathered through her, playing with her nerves and unpicking her composure, which had been pretty thin to start with.

'Which bit in particular are you talking about?'

Mia shrugged. 'You must have quite a busy social life. I mean…' she gave a smile that was a mix of reassuring, mildly interested and screamingly polite '…you've quizzed me about my youthful adventure with Kai but I don't even know whether there's someone back there in England waiting for you!' She shook her head with rueful apology and laughed. 'I guess you must be involved with someone and, if so, then I can only apologise for the fact that you're having to stay here longer than you'd anticipated.'

Outside, the steady pounding of the rain was like a background symphony.

'Why would you assume that I might be involved with someone?' Max eventually asked and this time, when she smiled, it was more genuine.

'Because…you're the kind of guy I guess certain types of women would be attracted to…'

'Certain types of women?' His eyebrows shot up and Mia blushed.

'Sorry. I didn't mean to offend you.' But what she *had* meant to do was deflect him from any suspicion that *she* might be one of those women.

'Firstly, you really need to stop apologising, and secondly, it would take a great deal more than that to offend me. I'm curious, however, to know what these certain types of women might be like.'

Mia bristled because she could tell that he was mocking her. However, she'd started the conversation, and now couldn't see a way of abandoning it. Besides, why not be honest? She was curious. Did he have a type? All men had a type. What was his? It was shameful just how curious she was.

'Sophisticated,' she said, head to one side, frowning in thought while surreptitiously watching him.

There was only one light on in the room and the mellow glow emphasised the harsh beauty of his features. He was so achingly perfect, from the curve of his sensual mouth to the brooding intensity of his deep navy, almost black eyes. He had one hand on his thigh and his legs were spread apart, inviting her to look at the way his jeans were pulled taut across muscular thighs.

'Sophisticated and glamorous,' she added breathlessly.

'Sophisticated...' Max murmured. 'Glamorous... Well, yes, I suppose those women *do* fit the broad spec.'

Of course they would, Mia thought sourly, although still smiling as she looked at him. Sophisticated, glamorous men always went for sophisticated, glamorous women. No big shocks to the system there!

'Although,' he continued, 'there's no one pining for me back in England. It's been a few weeks since I went out with anyone, as it happens.'

'I'm surprised you're not married,' Mia said in a clear breach of the employer-employee relationship she knew she should cling fast to.

He was the most guarded human being she

had ever met in her life. He couldn't have been more different from Izzy, from the way he looked to the way he acted, but then she was beginning to flesh out the bigger picture about their family dynamics.

He was the oldest, and he was the one who had been the powerhouse and decision maker of the family. She knew nothing about James, the mysterious middle child, the one Izzy absolutely adored, but she knew that Max had overseen his sister's movements with beady, watchful eyes. Wasn't that why she had ended up in charge of a hotel with a brief to kit it out just the way Max wanted? He had handed her a golden opportunity, just as long as it conformed to what he wanted, and if it didn't then he would not think twice about snatching back that golden opportunity.

He was a workaholic but even workaholics got married, had kids and assumed the mantle of a domestic life. Okay, a high-powered, rich-beyond-words domestic life, but even so...

The sophisticated guy would marry the sophisticated woman because that was always the next step on the ladder.

And Max Stowe was the epitome of drop-dead gorgeous sophistication. He oozed it from every pore. Women followed his movements out of the corner of their eyes and men tiptoed around him, in awe of that aura of powerful invincibility he seemed to radiate.

It had only been a handful of days, but she had seen enough to know that he controlled the world around him and everyone in it with an iron fist.

But she hadn't been kidding when she had let slip that she thought he lived a lonely life. She just couldn't help herself from wondering why he did.

'I don't pay you to be surprised about any aspect of my private life,' he murmured.

His words were like freezing water poured over her yet there was a darkening in his eyes when he spoke that made her skin tingle. He looked relaxed, lazy…and yet strangely alert. There was an undercurrent of sizzling sexuality in the air between them but she wasn't sure whether she was imagining it or not.

Of course you are. He just said that he liked sophisticated women...

'No. You don't...' Her voice hitched in her throat.

'But...' He shrugged and smiled slowly. 'It's no big secret that I don't do long-term relationships, far less marriage.'

'Why not?'

'Life's too short for the complications they bring.' His voice was deadly serious. 'I work hard and I'm only human. I enjoy having fun. But the fun stops when conversations about permanence begin.'

Mia was desperate to probe but the doorbell shattered the bubble they were in. She started and blinked as he vaulted upright and headed to the front door, waving her down, even though she didn't make a move to get to her feet.

He didn't do permanence. He didn't do long-term relationships. He would certainly have no sympathy for a sister who'd cut and run because of a broken affair. Strangely, the fact that he had not hauled Izzy back to make a case for herself was a credit to him. It showed that he had tried to see the bigger picture even though he fundamentally probably couldn't grasp it.

He returned with a selection of delicious looking food.

'I know the whereabouts of your kitchen,' he drawled, dumping the bags on the weathered coffee table he had dragged in front of the sofa where she was sitting. 'I'll bring in everything we need. You stay put. The less weight you put on that ankle, the faster it'll mend. Two days and you should be able to move around.'

The food was amazing. The conversation reverted to normal topics to do with the hotel. They talked about the budget that would be needed to landscape the grounds.

Her head was still buzzing with the taboo subject of his personal life, though…

Watching her as she ate, using the chopsticks like a pro, Max marvelled at a conversation that had veered wildly off course from the straight and narrow to the unpredictable and personal.

Being here, with the rain outside and darkness pressing against the windows, was like being in a cocoon. Being in this country was like being in a cocoon!

Real life with all its boundaries and restrictions was temporarily on hold.

He lowered his eyes, shielding his expression, but every pore and nerve in his body was tuned in to her as she delicately sampled the food straight from the boxes, making little noises of satisfaction that she probably wasn't even aware that she was making.

He'd brought over a couple of books from the bookshelf and stuck a cushion on top for a makeshift footstool. Her bandaged foot was propped on it, the other leg tucked under her. She was supple. She surfed! She was *going* to be supple!

The women he had dated in the past, those sophisticated women at whom he suspected Mia secretly sneered, largely abhorred anything to do with outdoor forms of exercise and swimming would have posed an impossible challenge. Their preferred form of exercise involved designer outfits and working out in a gym where they could see themselves in vast mirrors. Being soaked in open water would have sent them running for the hills. Those women seemed like a species from another planet.

Life on the other side of the pond was, what felt like, a million miles away.

The rigid parameters of his life were a million miles away…

He'd never had a break from being a tycoon. He knew that he was feared and respected in equal measure. From the age of twenty-two, he had made himself impregnable because he'd had no choice. To succeed in the hothouse of big business, you had to be tough, and being tough had come easily because he'd already had a head start in that area.

He'd been emotionally tough from the age

of ten and he'd learnt how to use that to his advantage.

Now, over a decade later, he was an iron man.

But suddenly, here…

He questioned whether he had become so isolated in his ivory tower and so focused on maintaining control over every aspect of his life, both emotionally and professionally, that he had managed successfully to eliminate every shred of spontaneous experience that didn't conform to his exacting rules.

Mia surprised and unsettled him. She wasn't afraid to speak her mind. She resented him helping her and was unimpressed with his money. She constantly pushed against the *Keep Out* signs and, instead of slamming the barriers down further, he hesitated. He hesitated because he was oddly invigorated by the novelty of having someone question him.

The fact that he fancied her added to the mix.

All told, a little novelty went a long way and he was jaded. Life in the city was lived in fifth gear. He barely noticed the cool luxury of his house in Holland Park, with its marble and glass and soft silk rugs, and Hockney and Lichtenstein pieces interspersed with more unknown originals. He seldom visited his places in Barbados and the Cotswolds, although he did stay at his penthouse in New York, largely because he went there on business a fair amount. He almost certainly wouldn't spend much time on the family yacht his brother had just bought.

In under a fortnight, he would return to his comfort zone but, for the first time, he wondered if this might not be a chance to step out of the box.

He glanced around him. He'd already half stepped out of the box just by being here. He hadn't been in a place like this for a long time. Never, when he thought about it.

He didn't do hanging out in women's houses but, even if he did, none of the houses would have resembled this one. This was a house filled with its occupant's personality. Every book on the bookshelf told a story. The two hardbacks under her foot were tomes on the virgin rainforests of Borneo and *Gardens that Changed the World,* respectively. Her kitchen was a riot of colour, with reminders stuck on the fridge under magnets. The furniture was old, soft and enveloping. There was not a hint of white, marble, chrome or glass anywhere to be seen.

The house reflected Mia.

It was as much a novelty for him as she was. His resolve never to mix business with pleasure began to fray at the edges.

'Molokai.'

Absorbed in the improbable meandering of his thoughts, Max surfaced to pick up what she had been saying about Izzy's plans for the hotel. 'What did you say?'

'Were you listening to a word I've been saying?'

Max muttered something and nothing. He'd been listening but most of what she had been saying had been sidelined by the more pressing business of watching the movement of her mouth and wondering what it might taste like.

Wondering what it might feel like to rebel against his own self-imposed restraints.

What it might feel like to take a walk on the wild side for a week...ten days, max...

'You were telling me why my ideas for the hotel were flushed down the toilet...'

'I was *telling* you that Izzy went to a lot of trouble to come up with what she felt would really work for tourists wanting to immerse themselves in the real feel of Hawaii and the islands.'

'Carry on. I'm all ears. How is your foot feeling?'

'Much better.' A brief hesitation. 'There's no need for you to stay here any longer. I can make my way to bed and I'll be fine in the morning.'

'Hardly fine enough to trek through the grounds of the hotel so that you can fill me in on all those plans in the making.'

'No. Maybe not.'

'Which is why you need to carry on. Fill me in right now on what Izzy had in mind, ease me in gently to the way my vision for the hotel has been roundly discarded...'

'Well, she did some travelling to the other islands... You know, each island has its own identity. All you've seen is this island and you've only seen a tiny bit of it, the bit that all the tourists see. You see the beach and the surfers and the restaurants and food trucks, but there's so much more to Hawaii than all of that, and that's what your sister was so interested in finding out about.'

'So much more...'

'I *know* you think that when it comes to an expensive hotel cold, soulless luxury is the only thing a rich clientele would be interested in...'

Max burst out laughing, and when he sobered up his eyes were alight with vibrant amusement.

'Not,' he said, grinning, 'that you would ever succumb to gross exaggeration...'

Mia smiled sheepishly and dipped her eyes. 'We worked on it together, really. I think she was impressed by my vision for an eco-

friendly outside space, with natural spots between the trees and shady areas bursting with
home-grown vegetables and herbs.'

'So she decided to do a bit of adventuring...
Did she also decide to stay put on one of the
other islands in search of inner peace after
her relationship ran aground?' He didn't expect her to answer that one and she didn't.
She was staunch in her loyalty and he ad-
mired that. Between them, the Chinese food
was beginning to congeal. He would see to
that later.

'There's no need for sarcasm,' Mia said
coldly.

'Absolutely none. Please. Continue. I'm all
ears.'

He gazed at her, utterly serious, and she
gazed right back at him with narrow-eyed
suspicion.

'She got inspiration from all the different
islands. Molokai... Maui... Kauai...'

'She...never said. I would never have
guessed,' Max said heavily. 'It's inspired. I
just wish she'd felt she had the freedom to

discuss it with me. No matter.' He began to stand, reaching for the containers and the plates, his voice brisk when he next spoke.

'And don't stand up. I'll clear this and then I'll make sure you're settled with some pain-killers to hand before I leave. And tomor-row...?' He paused and their eyes met. 'Well, it's time for me to see first-hand what you're talking about. I have the final say on what gets done on the hotel I'm paying for, but never let it be said that I'm not willing to see things from another angle.'

'And you'll go in with an open mind?'

'I'm taking it from that tone of voice that you're harbouring doubts about my sincer-ity...'

'Would you blame me?'

'I'm assuming that's a rhetorical question,' he drawled. 'But it's by the by, because the one way you can make absolutely sure that I give it a chance is to persuade me.'

'That's what I've just been trying to do!'

'I need more than persuasion from a sofa in your house, Mia. You tell me about all these inspirational islands…that's fine because you and I are going to travel to all of them and you can talk as much as you want about the vision my sister had for the hotel. And who knows? I might just buy into it…'

In the ensuing brief silence, he watched her face, and in his head, he thought, *What would it feel like to let go for once?*

CHAPTER SIX

THIS DIDN'T FEEL like work. Waiting nervously in her house, unable to relax but likewise unable to walk around because her bandaged foot was still hurting even though the sharp pain of the day before had eased, Mia had no idea how she had ended up agreeing to a four-day tour of the islands.

But, then again, how had she managed to end up confiding all sorts of personal details about her life to him? She rarely confided and she certainly never had heart-to-hearts with anyone about what had happened in her marriage. Had she been so distracted?

One minute, she had been solid in her determination to maintain a businesslike approach to their working relationship and, the next minute, he was carrying her into her house, dealing with a sprained ankle and somehow enticing confidences from her that should not have been revealed.

When she had closed her eyes the night before, she had been overwhelmed with an image of his dark head as he knelt at her feet and again she had felt that powerful urge to lace her fingers through his springy hair to see what it would feel like.

Now, waiting for him to show up at the time he'd said he would, her heart was leaping inside her and she had given up trying to project what this four-day sightseeing hop might look like.

When she started thinking about it, she had to ward off a panic attack, so she'd concluded that her best bet was to cross the bridge when she came to it.

He could have just given her time off work for her foot to heal, because wasn't that what any normal, considerate boss would have done in the circumstances? But, as he had said, time was money, and he didn't have a lot of time to play around with—not with England and his mega-high-powered life impatiently waiting for him. Plus, he was hardly the normal, considerate type, was he?

She just wished she could have felt more resentful, but as she waited for him to show up she couldn't quite subdue a simmering sense of excitement.

She had packed workman-like clothes. If he wanted to explore where Izzy's inspiration had come from, then he was going to be in for a shock, because he wouldn't be on a sightseeing tour of the usual tourist destinations and he wouldn't be taken to the sort of uber-luxurious hotels to which he was accustomed. Accordingly, she had packed a sturdy selection: two pairs of jeans and some cargo pants, tee shirts and hiking boots and thick hiking socks. She wasn't sure whether she would be up to any hiking boots scenario, but just in case…

He hadn't asked her what clothes to bring, so tough if he decided to pack stuff that was inappropriate.

When she thought about that, she couldn't resist smirking, but the tension was back full steam when, at a little after two in the after-noon, she heard the deep roar of his car as his driver pulled up outside her house.

The torrential rain of the day before had disappeared, replaced by the usual bright skies and warm sun. The weather here could be like that. All sound and fury one minute, gently caressing the next.

She opened the door and, even though she was well prepared, she still felt that automatic racing of her heart as she was confronted with him. Groundhog Day. That was what it was beginning to feel like. Whatever bracing talks she gave herself about self-control, one look at him and back she went to square one.

'How's the foot?'

Mia looked down then raised her eyes to his. 'Much better.'

'I've brought you this. Consider it a present.' He held out a fancy crutch. 'I'll obviously try to ensure that you put as little weight on your foot as possible, but that's not going to be possible much of the time.' He watched as she hoicked the crutch under her armpit. 'Unless,' he drawled, 'you want me to carry you…?'

'I'll be fine,' Mia said hurriedly.

He'd taken her rucksack and hoisted it over his shoulder.

He looked sinfully, wickedly sexy. Denim jeans, the usual tan loafers and a fitted, V-necked grey tee shirt that did amazing things for his body.

Mia averted her eyes. Somehow, in the muddle of being talked into this trip, she had failed to pin him down on the details, and as she settled into the back seat of the car she turned to him and said, urgently, 'I don't even know where exactly we'll be going…'

Max angled himself so that he was looking at her. 'To see a bit more of the islands,' he murmured. 'Wasn't that the recommended piece of advice so that I could have an idea of why all my dull and anodyne ideas were jettisoned? You told me that I needed to see the real Hawaii, so I'm just obeying orders.'

'I can't imagine you ever obeying orders,' Mia said under her breath, but not so quietly that he didn't pick it up, because he grinned and raised his eyebrows.

When he grinned like that, she thought distractedly, he was so...*engaging.* She could feel her natural defence mechanisms wobble a little. *Four days!* And she *still* didn't know what those four days were going to look like!

All about work, of course, because this wasn't a holiday, and he was a workaholic who would get his pound of flesh whatever the cost—but what was going to happen during downtime? There was only so much work they could reasonably be expected to do. What happened when the laptops got closed, the briefing was done and the accounts were put to bed? Even with his promise, she would remind him that after five her time would be her own to do with as she saw fit.

'Do you have an itinerary?' she asked briskly and frowned when he grinned a bit more.

'Of sorts.'

'What does that mean?'

'It means that I got someone to run through

what I should be expecting on the various islands and I made sure they sorted out our trip accordingly.'

'You got someone…?'

'Nat was very helpful, and his suggestions were reinforced by what the tourist guide at the hotel had to offer. In the absence of knowing anything about the place, I went with the flow and booked various venues accordingly.'

'You should have asked me,' Mia said accusingly and his grin widened.

Dammit, she wished he would stop doing that. It was all she could do not to be seduced into thinking that this was going to be *fun*, when his expression was light and his eyes were amused and the harsh, ruthless, arrogant self-assurance that wound her up so much was not in evidence.

'I would have done,' he said on a rueful, insincere sigh. 'But I thought it best for you to focus on recovering after your little mishap. We can talk about the itinerary when we board the plane to Maui. That's our first port of call.'

'You *do* know that Maui is nicknamed the Beverley Hills Island, don't you? Which is not exactly what I had in mind when it came to showing you the inspiration behind Izzy's reworking of the hotel.'

'But we have to start somewhere,' Max murmured. 'Actually, when it comes to luxury, we'll be starting somewhat sooner...'

He jerked his head and Mia—who had not taken in where they were going, or even how much distance they had been covering in the smoothly purring luxury car—now saw that, yes, they had certainly arrived at the airport. But this was not the section of the airport with which she was familiar.

They were being driven to a shiny black jet and her mouth dropped open in amazement.

'We're getting there in *this*?'

Max nodded, already swinging his long body out of the car while his driver sprang into action and pulled open her door. Hand on the bonnet of the car, he leant in and met her eyes. 'Less stressful than battling with the stampeding hordes at the airport.'

Impressed to death, she hobbled alongside him into the jet. It was ridiculously opulent, big enough to fit up to twelve people, but it was soon obvious that they would be the only occupants.

The seats were a rich, buttery cream leather, the tables were highly polished walnut and the pale tufted carpet made her want to kick off her sandals and riffle her toes through its soft pile. Champagne was offered by a smiling, uniformed young woman. Mia shook her head. Max, barely glancing at either the woman or the tray, grabbed a glass in passing but he was already on the phone as they settled into their seats.

Mia realised that he was completely oblivious to his surroundings. He could have been on a bus for all the attention he paid to the luxurious jet.

The differences between them gaped wide. The differences between him and his sister were even more puzzling, given they both came from the same background.

She settled into the seat and gazed around

her. Agenda? Itinerary? She had to drag her mind back to reality as she waited for him to finish his phone call.

Half listening, she realised that he was talking to his brother about a yacht. Had they just bought one? The level of wealth was mind-boggling.

'It's so weird.' She turned to him as soon as he was off the phone and he looked at her quizzically.

'Leading statement,' he said. 'Can't wait to hear where this is going.'

'All of this…' She made a sweeping gesture to encompass the jet, the flute of champagne, the leather, and the walnut and the hush. Because the young woman who had handed them drinks had tactfully faded into the background and the pilot was still on the ground, talking to whomever pilots of private jets needed to talk before they took off. 'You're not impressed, are you?'

He looked absently around him and shrugged. 'I stopped being impressed by the things money can buy a long time ago. When it comes to private jets, I've been on many, and many were bigger, faster and better-looking.'

'You're so different from Izzy.'

'So I'm beginning to conclude.'

'I mean…' Mia frowned and placidly bypassed the unwelcoming expression on his face. 'Of course I knew from the start that she came from a wealthy background, because she told me that she had been hired by you to handle the hotel as a first job experience. How many girls are blessed enough to cut their teeth on such a great job? But, if I hadn't known that, if I'd just met her out and about, there's no way I would ever have thought that she came from money.'

'Because…? And I ask because I don't suppose there's the slightest chance of closing this conversation down until you've said what you intend to.'

Mia was vaguely aware of an impatient edge to his voice, but she was a lot more aware of his forearm resting close to hers on the arm rest of the seat. Her eyes kept straying to its sinewy strength, the length of his fingers, the dark, fine hair.

'Because she never dresses in designer clothes and she honestly doesn't seem impressed by the fact that she can pretty much have whatever she wants. I guess, judging from all of this...'

'I'll have to take your word on that,' Max intoned abruptly. 'I can't say I've ever paid much attention to the clothes my sister wore.'

The pilot was now in the plane and he walked over, shook hands and chatted about the flight. He inspired confidence. It was a relief, because Mia had never been in anything as small as this before. She could surf with the best of them, and the ocean didn't scare her, but on the three occasions when she had flown on a plane she had been sickly nervous of the fact that the ground was nowhere near beneath her. Now, peering out of the circular window, she had disturbing visions of being in a matchbox high up in the air, tossed about by air currents. Her stomach swooped.

She'd been talking about Izzy but now, as

the pilot headed towards the cockpit, the conversation was lost in a wave of high-wire tension.

'I've never been on a private jet before.' Her voice was unnaturally high and she cleared her throat.

'I gathered,' Max said wryly.

'No. I mean I've never…' She breathed in deeply as the engines roared into deafening life. She wished she had some vital statistics to hand. How many of these tiny little pieces of metal fell from the sky every year? Maybe, in this instance, ignorance was bliss. 'I mean…' She clutched the arms of the chair in a death-defying grip. 'I've never been up in the air in anything quite as small as this…'

'Are you okay?'

'Absolutely!'

As the plane began to taxi, she felt her nerves begin to shred even though she told herself that this was probably safer for getting from A to B than some of the taxis she occasionally took after she'd been out at night.

It might feel as fragile as a paper plane, but it was as sturdy as a rock. Surely?

'What's wrong?' Max asked sharply.

'I feel a little sick.'

'Jesus. Are you *scared*?'

'No,' Mia squeaked.

'Look at me!'

She stared straight at him as the jet shot upwards at what felt like supersonic speed. She felt a rocket couldn't have gone faster. Her insides were all over the place and she wanted to whimper even though her head was telling her to behave.

Two things happened at once. She squeezed her eyes tightly shut and...he kissed her.

He kissed her!

It was so unexpected that Mia's eyes flew open in shock. His mouth on hers was a drug, obliterating everything. She felt the warm dart of his tongue against hers and she sighed, succumbed to the kiss, succumbed to something she realised she'd been fantasising about practically from the first moment she'd clapped eyes on him.

And nothing could have prepared her for how sweet it would be. How much she would want it to go on and on, for ever. There was no space inside her for fear.

The hand that been clutching the armrest crept up, tangling in that luxurious dark hair, and the other hand somehow managed to find the curve of his cheek.

She felt her breasts tingling, her nipples spiking against her bra, and she was wet, so wet, between her thighs.

He was cupping her face and playing with her ear with one finger. The tiny movements sent electric currents racing through her body, lighting up every part of her, as though she'd suddenly been plugged into a live socket.

Then just like that he pulled away and cold air filled the void.

It took a couple of seconds for Mia to snap out of her daze.

'You should be all fine now,' he murmured, sending her one last look before sitting back and finishing the glass of champagne.

'All fine? What? Oh!' Of course. He'd

kissed her and she'd lost herself in it like a teenager in the full throes of adolescent lust. Her lips tingled from where his had been and every pore in her body was buzzing with energy. She wanted to touch her mouth with her hand, and she made sure she didn't give in to any such temptation by firmly clasping them together on her lap.

She'd been terrified as the jet had soared at a vertical angle into the clouds and he'd kissed her to distract her from the terror. He'd seen it writ large on her face and he'd kindly gone for a swift remedy, and it had worked because she had yielded to that kiss and enjoyed every second of it.

Humiliation roared through her. She went hot, then cold, then she shook her head and rolled her eyes and cracked a smile.

'I should thank you.'

Their eyes collided and for a few seconds Max remained silent, his expression veiled.

The last thing he'd considered doing when he'd hit Hawaii in search of his wayward sister was making an impromptu tour of islands he wasn't remotely interested in visiting.

That said, the last thing he'd expected was a woman furiously digging her feet in and denying him the information he had travelled thousands of miles to obtain. And, from there, everything else had been a slow unravelling of life as he knew it.

What he *did* know was that he'd never felt more invested in having this woman.

It was a weakness. He knew that. He loathed the way it undermined his hard-headed logic, but it was an overpowering urge he couldn't seem to fight.

He'd seen her today dressed in her usual 'day at a building site' uniform, and he'd smiled, because no one could accuse her of putting herself out to dress up for him.

Indeed, what she wore was an act of defiance.

He wondered how she would react if she knew just how sexy she was in shapeless cargo pants and a pair of flat sandals, with her hair tied back in a ponytail.

Her beauty was luminescent.

And his body had reacted accordingly. He'd breathed her in as she'd settled into the seat next to him and, of course, predictably, she had entertained him with her forthright, no-holds-barred, uninvited insights into his personal life.

Was it because he'd expected her mouthy, outspoken, full-frontal attack and her sudden panic on the plane had driven him to do what he'd been longing to do for days? Their eyes had met, he'd seen the utterly soft and vulnerable fear there and he'd thought of one thing and one thing only. Kissing her. Kissing that fear out of existence. Kissing her until she forgot everything but *him*.

She'd melted into him and her soft acquiescence had sent his libido shooting into the stratosphere. For the first time in his life, his self-control had been utterly and completely obliterated.

And that had scared the hell out of him.

It was one thing musing thoughtfully about breaking his own self-imposed rules about never mixing business with pleasure. It was one thing contemplating tasting the freedom of straying out of his comfort zone. It was quite another to discover that he just hadn't been able to help himself. His body had taken the decision-making out of his hands, and that had never happened before.

Yet now, even as he sensed her withdrawing at speed, covering up the fact that she had enjoyed that kiss as much as he had, he itched to pull her right back into him and carry on where they had left off.

He could have her. In that moment, he had sensed her want, had known what he had suspected…

But hard on the heels of that pleasing recognition came one that was slightly less welcome.

Lust was one thing but the thought of distancing himself and denial in the aftermath… A moment's pleasure was never worth an hour of post-pleasure angst and guilt, and some inner radar was telling him that post-pleasure angst and guilt might be her natural response.

'Thank me? For the distraction?' He shot her a crooked, amused smile and didn't take his eyes off her flushed face. 'Did you enjoy it?' he murmured, voice low and husky.

'It did the job,' she returned crisply, which made him smile more. Where most women would have offered seconds, she could barely meet his eyes. He felt back in control and that split-second of disturbing unease had been banished. In fact, he felt buoyant.

'In that case, glad to be of service.'

'Tell me about the itinerary.'

'The itinerary...'

'Where *exactly* we're going and where we'll be staying and other such things.'

'I have a printout somewhere.' If she ran any faster from acknowledging that kiss, then she'd be in danger of tripping over her own feet in her haste.

'Perhaps I could see it?'

'We could always wait until we get to the

hotel,' he drawled. 'Review it in more relaxed conditions. It's a short flight.'

Flustered, Mia chewed her lip. She was still so unsettled she could barely think clearly. Bringing things back to business should have worked, should have focused her mind, but he wasn't playing ball, and she was at a loss as to how to drag the conversation back to where she wanted it.

Did you enjoy it...?

What kind of question was *that*? she inwardly fumed. He'd been laughing at her. She was sure of it. She'd done her best to act cool and collected but, not to beat about the bush, she'd practically hurled herself into his arms the second his mouth had touched hers. He was a guy with a lot of experience, and he would have had to be blind to miss the shameful enthusiasm of her response. Of course he was laughing at her now! Did he think that she had seriously imagined that he actually fancied her? Yes. Yes, he did.

'I don't even know what hotel you've booked.'

'You'll like it. Trust me.' He grinned and she returned a withering look because she was pretty sure she wasn't going to like what he said next, not judging from the barely contained laughter in his navy eyes. 'Or maybe not… You might find it just more tedious luxury after you've been forced to endure the horror of a private jet.'

'I never said that this was horrible!'

'I know, but somehow you've managed to remind me at every turn that my life choices are too materialistic and therefore leave a lot to be desired.'

Mia sniffed. He didn't sound offended. He sounded amused. The wretched man sounded *relaxed* while she, on the other hand, was in state of churning, inner turmoil.

'I'm very sorry if that was the impression I gave,' she said coolly.

'No, you're not.' He was still grinning. 'If it's one thing you're never sorry about, it's giving me a headache.'

'That's not true!' She bristled.

'I like it,' Max murmured softly.

Wrong-footed for the second time in as many minutes, Mia shot him a nonplussed look from under her lashes.

'I can't believe you're lost for words.'

'I… I…'

'I'm surrounded by people who aim to please. It's refreshing to be in the company of someone who aims to criticise.'

'I don't…aim to criticise…'

He liked it? He found it refreshing?

Mia stifled a sudden rush of pleasure. He found her refreshing? Since when? He certainly hadn't found her refreshing when she'd refused to disclose his sister's whereabouts.

And then…when he'd kissed her…

Had there been more to that kiss than a perfunctory desire to stop her from going into a full-blown meltdown?

Mia had been too long in the game of being careful to let her head be swayed by some good-looking guy with a few well-chosen, softly spoken words. Wasn't she? She was a down-to-earth girl from a down-to-earth family who wanted a down-to-earth guy.

When it came to relationships, she was serious. Even though her marriage had crashed and burned, she and Kai had both been on the same page when it had come to wanting the joy of lasting commitment. They just hadn't been able to find that with one another.

All this sizzling excitement that filled her when she was within touching distance of this guy counted for nothing. It was a little reminder that she was flesh and blood with urges just like the next person which, given the fact that she had been in a physical deep freeze for way too long, was fantastic. But, in the end, that was all it was.

If she allowed her imagination to get too carried away, then she would be making a grave mistake, betraying all those principles she had been brought up to hold dear. Not going to happen.

Which brought her back to the importance of grounding the conversation before it developed a momentum of its own.

'This all happened very fast.' She was bolt upright in the leather seat and, although she wasn't looking at him, she could feel his eyes lazily watching her. She fancied that he could detect every shift in her posture, in her voice, in her expression. 'And I didn't have much time to lay down any ground rules.'

Was it possible to feel someone's eyebrows shoot up?

'Ground rules?'

'Yes.' She angled herself so that she was looking at him but immediately regretted that because now all she could focus on was his beautiful mouth. Her eyes flicked up to meet his. 'And, before you tell me that I work for you, I need to remind you that my hours are nine to five.'

'No need to remind me.'

Mia licked her lips. 'We can work out an agenda for during the day, and I'll do that just as soon as I get to the hotel, but at five my working day ends and I… I think it's only fair that I be permitted to do my own thing.'

'I wouldn't dream of handcuffing you to my side and forcing you to work strictly to rule.'

'Good.'

'I expect you know the islands well?'

'I've been to a couple of them,' Mia said, relaxing, because at last here was a conversation she could run with. 'In fact, I spent a few days showing Izzy around when she mentioned that she wanted to see more than just Oahu and Honolulu. She was very much interested in getting off the beaten track. Not that you could ever say that bits of Maui were off the beaten track.' She smiled. 'I guess you'll want to see more than just the touristy side of the islands,' she said. 'We could hire a tour guide.'

'We could do that,' Max murmured, non-committal. 'We'll discuss all of that when we get to the hotel and start going through the nuts and bolts of how this is going to play out. Tell me what I can expect.'

'What you can expect?'

'I've never been to this part of the world before.'

Mia leaned back against the seat and half closed her eyes and watched flashbacks from her past. Growing up with the ocean a stone's throw away… Learning to swim and then, when she'd been barely able to walk, being introduced to a baby surf board… The rowdy pleasure of coming from a large family and the numerous picnics and camping weekends they had enjoyed… Her love of the lush greenery and her determination to try her hand at an outdoor life, to explore that side of her that loved nature in defiance of her sisters, who had all entered various professions… When she had started helping Izzy with the 'boring paperwork', as she had called it, it had come as a surprise to discover that she rather enjoyed it.

The jet was landing by the time she had finished talking.

'You should have stopped me.' She blushed and looked at him a little guiltily. 'I've been babbling.'

'Vital information,' Max murmured. 'Right. Hold tight. We're landing. Grab my hand if nerves get the better of you.'

'Taking off is a lot worse,' Mia confided. 'At least there's ground beneath us when we land.' But she didn't shake off his hand when he covered hers with his. In fact, she liked it there, liked the way it made her feel safe.

Four days in the grand scheme of things was not even a blink of an eye.

Stick to work…quit at five…and everything would be fine.

She was barely aware, as the jet shuddered to a stop, of squeezing his hand, or of feeling the infinitesimal pressure as he returned the gesture.

CHAPTER SEVEN

THE HOTEL WAS the last word in opulence. It was perfectly positioned to gaze majestically down at the ocean, interrupted only by meticulously beautiful landscaped gardens, in the middle of which was a huge kidney-shaped swimming pool.

A long, black BMW was waiting for them as they left the jet. From luxury to more luxury, Mia thought.

She was being offered a rare glimpse into how the seriously rich lived and she was guiltily aware that a person could get used to this. It certainly beat tramping through airports, hunting down bags on carousels and then wending your way on public transport in searing heat, dragging a case behind you and apologizing every five steps because you'd accidentally crashed into someone.

Surrounded by birds of paradise as they approached the cool, marble dream of the hotel foyer, Mia tried to forget the dress-down utilitarian outfit she had chosen to wear. She sternly reminded herself that this was work. She wasn't on holiday. She wasn't going to be lounging by the side of a pool, summoning waiters over for cocktails. Indeed, she hadn't even brought a swimsuit with her.

Max was making sure to stick by her side, conscious of the fact that she wasn't quite back on her feet yet, and as soon as they got their respective keys he urged her to go upstairs and relax.

'You can meet me in the bar at six,' he said. 'We can grab a drink, an early dinner and go over the schedule for the next few days.'

Mia hesitated. Wherever she looked, she saw glamour. Designer clothes, designer luggage and so many designer sunglasses that she wondered giddily whether she had stepped into a spy movie.

Max fitted in perfectly without even trying. His clothes were positively shabby in comparison, and yet he looked more sophisticated than everyone around them. It was the way he carried himself and that way he had of implying that he just didn't care what anyone thought. He played by his own rules.

It was his 'leader of the pack' aura that turned heads and she saw very many swivelling surreptitiously in his direction.

She headed up, leaving him in the foyer, to discover that her room adjoined his and was connected by a door that was locked but presumably could be unlocked.

It was a magnificent space, with a sitting area, a small open-plan kitchenette and vast glass doors that led out onto a private balcony with spectacular views of the ocean. The bathroom was as big as a dance floor, with a bowl-shaped, free-standing tub and a walk-in shower with so many various knobs that she wondered whether she would be able to make sense of it without a manual.

The pain in her foot had eased sufficiently to allow her comfortably to undress and she took her time with a bath.

Her bag had been brought to her room prior to her entering, and unpacking it was a depressing reminder that, while she had been privately smug at the thought of Max not being properly equipped for anything other than luxury, she had failed to consider that she might be poorly equipped for anything other than outdoor casual.

In a short denim skirt and white tee shirt, which had seemed just the ticket for exploring on her own and eating in cheap local eateries, she now felt horrendously under-dressed. And half hobbling with a crutch under one arm didn't help matters when it came to her self-confidence as she later found her way to the bar.

It was a big hotel, with a bewildering amount of rooms on the ground floor and several restaurants dotted in various locations. Mia thought that there should have been an option to download satnav when they'd arrived because you needed it in a place as big as this.

It was a relief when she made it to the bar only ten minutes late, and she spotted him immediately. He was working, frowning in front of his laptop, completely oblivious to his surroundings and with a drink of some kind on the table next to him.

How did he do that? she wondered. How did he manage to look so carelessly elegant without even trying? How was it that, in an expensive bar filled with expensive-looking people, he stood out?

She took a deep breath and threaded her way towards him.

She'd hoped that his attention might remain on whatever was on the screen, but no such luck. He turned to watch as she slowly moved towards him.

Mia had been embarrassed at her outfit before, but she was red-faced and flustered by the time she slowly levered herself into the chair next to his.

'I'm—I'm sorry I'm a bit late,' she stuttered, feeling the hot burn of self-consciousness in her neck and face. 'And apologies,' she continued stiffly, 'but I'm afraid I didn't bring the required wardrobe for a place like this...'

Why on earth had she just said that? Why had she drawn attention to what she was wearing? Of course, she knew why. She felt horribly out of place and the words had shot out of her mouth before she'd had time to think them through.

Max looked around him, as though only now noticing the shameless luxury of their surroundings.

Then his navy eyes rested on her thoughtfully.

Mia bristled defensively, bracing herself for something caustic. Would it be too much to remind him that she was a *gardener* by profession, accustomed to working outdoors? Maybe she could remind him that this was a work situation, so who cared what she wore? Her role wasn't to look like an ornament.

'Does that bother you?' he asked mildly.

'No, of course not,' Mia lied unconvincingly.

'Of course it does. Why wouldn't it? Women

look at other women. It would be strange if you didn't find it discomforting to think that you might not be blending in.'

Mia heartily wished that she had kept her mouth shut. But she hadn't, which didn't mean she intended to indulge any long sermons about the stupidity of peer pressure.

She peered down at the drinks menu and made a deal of deciding what she wanted.

'A glass of white wine,' she said when someone materialised to take their order.

He ordered a bottle and rattled off a list of things for them to pick at.

'An early night.' He shrugged. 'Unless you would rather go to the restaurant?'

And just like that Mia knew that he had ordered bar food to spare her having to go to the Michelin-starred restaurant in clothes she'd admitted she felt uncomfortable wearing, and he'd done it without making a fuss.

Something inside her swooped and, when she smiled, it was with genuine warmth and just the merest hint of gratitude.

Nothing was said but their eyes met for a

few seconds, and for one moment they were perfectly attuned and on the same page.

It was an effort to remain neutral and professional for the remainder of the evening. The drinks came, the bar food arrived and they talked about the forthcoming agenda.

Maui and Kauai. One stunning and luxurious, the other equally stunning and perfect for nature-lovers. Lack of time dictated that exploring the rest of the islands would have to be put on the back burner.

'I never knew my sister was a nature lover,' he mused as the plates were taken away with a flourish.

After having drunk two glasses of wine, Mia returned honestly, 'It's not that hard to think you know someone only to find that you don't know them nearly as well as you thought you did.'

'By which, I take it, you're referring to your ex-husband?'

Where that would normally have sent her rapidly into reverse, drawing up the bridges to avoid an awkward conversation, the wine had relaxed her, along with that fleeting moment when she had warmed to the streak of empathy and understanding she had glimpsed in him.

There was only the vaguest recognition, somewhere on the periphery of her brain, that he really had an excellent memory. Also… just how much had she been lulled into confiding? And how had he managed to wriggle underneath her barriers, considering they had nothing in common and most of the time she didn't even like him?

She thought of that kiss when he had wanted to distract her…and her skin heated up at speed and she was lost for words for a few seconds.

How had they ended up talking about Kai? Where did her failed marriage fit into a conversation about the islands they intended to visit?

'That's the problem with marriage,' Max murmured into the lengthening silence. 'It ends up throwing up all sorts of problems that you never thought could possibly exist and, before you know it, what started off as the perfect fail-safe relationship degenerates into a train crash.'

'Not always. My parents have been happily married for nearly thirty-five years.'

'Which makes it all the more surprising.'

'Surprising? What's surprising?' When she looked at her glass, it was to find that it was empty. Her brain felt foggy and she was so alert to his presence that the rush of blood in her veins was an unwelcome reminder of the dramatic effect he had on her, against all odds.

'That you haven't sought to move on.'

'Who says I haven't?'

'Have you?'

'I've had other things on my mind.'

'So no one has come along to relieve you of those "other things"?'

'I've been on a couple of dates, but I'm not interested in jumping back into the water.'

'Maybe you just haven't met anyone com-pelling enough to encourage you to test the temperature.'

Mia looked away. Her pulse was racing, and for the life of her she couldn't work out how this guy could get her to say stuff she would normally never reveal.

To go deeper into this conversation would open up all sorts of confusing avenues. He didn't belong in any of those avenues. He didn't belong anywhere in her life except on a professional basis as her boss.

And yet, the atmosphere sizzled between them, fragmenting her thoughts and turning the ground beneath her feet into quicksand.

'Tomorrow…' she said, and he looked at her for a few seconds in silence before nodding.

'Tomorrow, work begins!'

'So I should head up now, if that's all right with you?' She began to stand so that he would get the message loud and clear and he waved his hand in easy dismissal.

Max watched her retreat. Her blushing admission about her outfit had not surprised him. Despite the feisty exterior and the almost complete inability to refrain from saying what was on her mind, with or without encouragement from him, she was oddly vulnerable at times, and in her vulnerability so intensely feminine.

And so unbelievably sexy.

He'd followed her progress as she'd made her way towards him and, if he'd wanted her two days ago, he wanted her more now. Released from his own self-imposed restrictions on having any kind of relationship with an employee, was his mind now taking advantage to wander freely?

He had been aware of her in the back of the car as they'd been driven to the hotel, and he'd had to drag his thoughts out of the realm of fantasy.

In this hotel, with its contingent of preening women in designer clothes, she had stood out, her natural beauty marking her out from the crowd, and the fact that she couldn't see that was both bewildering and touching at the same time.

It roused a protective urge in him that was halfway between amusing and unsettling.

Two hours after she had retired, and after a

series of calls and emails to CEOs involved in various levels of delicate deal-making in various countries, he retreated to his bedroom.

Her room was next to his, separated by a door. A locked one, admittedly, but the mere fact that a single door separated them played into the fantasies revolving in his head.

The room was icy, thanks to the air-conditioning, but despite that he fancied he could still feel the heat outside, slowing down his reactions and turning his thoughts in directions not taken before.

He had failed to arrange a time to meet the next day and he wasn't shocked when she texted bright and early the following morning to tell him that she would take breakfast in her room.

'Why?' He bypassed the dreary, long-winded business of texting her back and ended up calling her.

'Just washed my hair…couldn't possibly get it dried in time…removing the bandage from my foot…just wanted to hobble without the crutch in private to see how it felt…'

Blah, blah, blah.

'Meet me in the foyer.' He glanced at his watch, cutting through whatever further excuses might have been waiting in the wings. 'In an hour.'

There were a couple of things he needed to do, and both afforded him a great deal of satisfaction.

He was waiting for her when she made it to the foyer bang on time. The travelling outfit had been replaced by one almost identical, bar a slightly different range of colours. Did anyone really need a pair of trousers with enough pockets to hold everything bar the kitchen sink? Surely not?

He rose smoothly from where he was sitting and headed towards her.

Mia paused fractionally. She'd made her excuses with breakfast, having decided to take time out to remind herself that they were here for business, not pleasure.

Sadly, the very second she clapped eyes on him her heart skipped a beat, her mouth went dry and her eyes became nailed to his face.

Surely she couldn't be falling for this guy? Surely common sense would have prevented that? And yet there was an unescapable awareness that something inside her was being handed over to him… Surely it couldn't be her heart?

She gave a rictus smile and indicated her foot.

Keep it casual. Polite conversation whenever you're not talking about work-related matters…

'So much better,' she said when she was in front of him. 'I still have the crutch, but you were right. It was just an uncomfortable sprain. Probably not even that. Anyway, definitely on the mend! I took a couple of tablets first thing and I can almost walk on it.'

'Excellent news,' he murmured.

'Have you got an itemised plan for how the day is going to play out?'

'I certainly have.'

Mia, waiting for clarification, was disconcerted when he cupped her elbow and began gently ushering her away from the revolving glass door that led outside.

'Where are we going?' She looked behind her with consternation as he continued to guide her back into the hotel.

'You were uncomfortable with what you were wearing in the bar,' he said. 'You're not going to feel any more comfortable in the restaurant tonight.'

'Wh-why would I be in the restaurant?' Mia stuttered on a tide of rising panic.

'Where else do you plan on eating?'

'Out! After work...after five...having a look around...'

'Exploring an island on a crutch isn't the cleverest of ideas, is it?'

'It's on the mend!'

'And that's exactly how we want to keep it! Don't forget, you're here to do a job, and that job is going to be considerably easier if you can walk comfortably on that foot of yours— and hours outside in the baking heat, trying to find places to eat while hobbling from one café to another, just isn't going to do. I need you to be up and moving as fast as possible.'

Mia scowled.

'You still haven't explained…'

'Here we are,' he said with notable satisfaction.

It was a measure of how absorbed she was with him that she only belatedly registered that he was guiding her gently but firmly towards the bank of expensive shops nestled in the heart of the hotel.

Mia had no idea what was going on and she certainly wasn't about to be led anywhere like a sheep. 'Here where?' she questioned politely. 'I'm seeing a shop.'

'You didn't feel comfortable in the clothes you brought with you—' he shrugged expansively '—so we're going to change that.'

'Please don't tell me what I will and won't be doing!'

'A handful of outfits.' He shrugged. 'Pick what you like.'

'I don't need a handful of outfits!'

'And I don't need to be the object of avid curiosity because you're making a scene.'

Mia's eyes slid to where two elegant saleswomen were watching their antics, although they immediately averted their eyes when spotted.

Where Max could brush off that sort of thing, because he honestly didn't give a damn, *she* couldn't. She hadn't been raised that way. Other people's opinions *mattered* to her.

'This is ridiculous.' She tried to make her protest as cool and collected as possible. 'Furthermore, I can't afford anything from a place like this.'

'Do you imagine for a single second that I would allow you to pay for anything from this place? You're here because of me and I intend to cover all the costs.'

Their eyes met and held for a few seconds. There was no way she could express what she felt. How could she articulate that? That choosing clothes to have dinner with him felt dangerously intimate?

'Don't fight me on this, Mia.'

Mia glanced towards the elegant boutique and made a decision. 'Fine.' She shrugged and looked at him squarely. 'If you think it's necessary for me to have a new wardrobe, then I'll get a new wardrobe, but I'm a big girl and perfectly capable of choosing my own clothes. So, if you want to arrange a time and a place to meet, I can join you later.'

She pulled out her phone to check the time, crisply arranged when to meet and watched as he raked his fingers through his hair before nodding wryly.

It was an experience, what could be done with a bottomless bank account in a very expensive boutique. Mia was hardly aware of what was being chosen because the eager shop owner, having marvelled at her figure, proceeded to turn her into a mannequin for the next hour. At last, dazed, Mia was standing in front of an array of black and gold bags, that conveniently would be sent to her room so she didn't have the bother of carrying anything, and wondering what, exactly, she had purchased in the flurry of things being tried on.

'How was the torture chamber?' were Max's first words when she met him at the designated place.

'It was fine!' Mia said. She knew that she had been dragged way out of her comfort zone. In her world of surfing, landscaping and working in the open air, she had been able to shun fancy, girly-girl clothes, faintly scorning the preoccupation of the prom queen types who only cared about how they looked.

She was forced to concede that she had actually enjoyed the experience, and even more so when she guiltily thought of him looking at her in her new-fangled get-ups. Surely she couldn't be that shallow?

They settled into the back of the car he had commissioned for his personal use as and when. The scenery they looked at as they drove along the uncrowded roads was scenery that was in her blood. Overhanging trees, lush and in colours of every shade of green, over-sized bushes awash with purple and red flowers, fringing the road in bursts of vibrant colour. It rained a lot on this island, she explained, hence the lushness of the foliage.

The driver was an expert tour guide, who could name every tree and flower, and Mia found herself competing with him about who knew more, even though she was still so aware of Max sprawled beside her.

They crossed one-way bridges and they opened the windows, breathing in the warm breeze. He asked a lot of questions, and it was just as well, because it established a bit of normality between them after his earlier provocative remarks.

If only she could truly relax! She had been to the island many times and she directed them to the Halfway to Hana café, where they indulged in banana bread and shave ice. It was on a busy beach, with lots of noise and music. She vaguely remembered feeling smug at the thought of him in surroundings just like this— sitting in a hot café and being jostled on all sides, informal and brash, with loud music and lots of people and food to be eaten without knives and forks. Yet, when she looked at him, he couldn't have appeared more at ease in his surroundings.

She heard herself jabbering away about all manner of things throughout the course of the day, and it was blessed relief when at last they were back at the hotel at a little after four.

'Meet me at seven,' he told her, naming one of the fancy restaurants in the hotel as she was about to head to the lift, leaving him behind. There were few minutes in the day when he wasn't working and the day's outing had taken up quite a few of those precious minutes.

Back in her hotel room, she forgot what she'd hastily picked in the boutique. She pulled out the assortment of clothes and it was almost as though she was seeing most of them for the first time.

Her hand hovered over a dark blue shift... and then veered away to something smaller and more figure-hugging in just the sort of bold pattern she wouldn't usually wear...but loved the look of.

She used to wear dresses like that…

Back in the day. Before, she suddenly realised, a broken marriage had instilled a level of reserve she never really used to have.

Once upon a time, she used to laugh a lot more, wear brightly coloured clothes and let her hair lie long and loose over her shoulders and down her back.

Suddenly pierced with nostalgia, she stuck on the dress and looked at herself in the mirror, and was startled when someone much younger looked back at her.

Where had that girl gone and how had she not noticed her absence?

Mia made her way down to the restaurant. She carried the crutch, but she didn't really need it, and she almost regretted having brought it along because it felt like a prop.

The restaurant was small and intimate, and yet busy. Waiters buzzed around with huge circular trays. The atmosphere was casual, but nothing could quite disguise the fact that it was a mega-expensive venue. There was something about the tasteful pale green of the walls, the soft, faded silk rugs underfoot, the crisp white linen of the table cloths and the mellow lighting…

She saw him as instantly as she'd seen him in the bar the evening before. This time, he was dressed more formally in a white, short-sleeved shirt and a pair of charcoal-grey trousers. He looked so heart-stoppingly masculine that she faltered for a few seconds and then powered on.

Max had managed to secure the perfect table in a corner of the room, and he watched her progress with a veiled expression. He'd been waiting for fifteen minutes in a state of keen anticipation that was uncool, to say the least.

Why the hell was he playing with fire? Since when had that been a recommended game for a guy who exerted such control over every aspect of his life?

But today it had been torture, being with her for hours, breathing in her fresh, floral scent, his eyes stubbornly lingering on her startlingly pretty face.

He had given up trying to rein in his imagination.

He wanted her. It was something he couldn't quite explain to himself.

Maybe if he hadn't sensed that chemistry between them, hadn't tasted the softness of her mouth or watched the hungry flick of her eyes when she thought she was unnoticed... But he had and it fired him in ways that were shocking.

Now, watching, he felt the hot rush of blood heavy in his veins.

She was wearing a dress and it was the first time he'd seen her in one.

She looked so...*delectable*. He breathed in slowly, taming his body. He didn't play games when it came to women but now... this...felt like a game, a dangerous game, and he couldn't wait for the starting gun to be fired.

CHAPTER EIGHT

AFTERWARDS, MIA WAS hard-pressed to figure out just when the atmosphere between them had shifted.

The dress had done something for sure, flicked a switch in her head, because as she walked towards him, barely using the crutch at all, she felt like a million dollars. The brush of cool silk against her skin was seductive. And then his eyes…veiled and hooded…as he watched her get closer.

The food was amazing and there was champagne.

And the conversation was so work-orientated as he plied her with questions about bits of the island they hadn't got round to seeing. They discussed the various financing avenues for some of the plans his sister had begun to put in place. They worked out what would make sense and what wouldn't. More champagne was poured. He all but brought out his laptop so that they could study costs and projected revenues.

It was a conversation that should have relaxed her, because it reinforced the status quo between them without her having to remind herself of it every five seconds.

But behind the affable exchange of ideas, and discussion of timetables and supply chains, there was the steady pulse of something else, something she glimpsed just like a shadow, when she felt the brush of his knee against hers under the table or caught the glitter of guarded amusement in his eyes and in the curve of his mouth.

Another conversation was being had under the surface and it was *exciting.*

She liked it. She liked the fizz of the champagne, the fizz of excitement running through her veins, the quiet, casual elegance of their surroundings and the shiver of not quite knowing what was going to happen when the evening drew to an end.

As it was doing now. They floated from the restaurant to the bank of lifts, purring up to their floor.

'So...' Max drawled, staring at the brushed steel of the lift door. 'What do you think of the accommodation?'

'My room?'

'Like it?' He shifted to glance over at her.

'It's the nicest hotel room I've ever stayed in—not that there have been very many. Of course, when it comes to delivering on the sort of atmosphere Izzy had in mind for—'

'I'm not interested in talking about my sister or what she happened to have in mind.'

'I just thought...' The doors pinged open and here they were, in the wide marble and walnut corridor leading to their adjoining rooms.

'We've spent the past two hours talking about work,' Max murmured. 'We now have two minutes before we reach our rooms to talk about what we both really wanted to talk about over that dinner.'

Mia's heart sped up. She wasn't looking at

him, but she could feel him with every pore in her body. Then their eyes met and held. She had a choice to make. A fierce longing tore into her, and as it did common sense and prudence, two of her loyal companions when it came to her emotions, began to shrivel under the hot glare of her simmering excitement.

She was young! Didn't she *deserve* to have a bit of reckless fun for once in her life?

She had never anticipated this sledgehammer kind of lust, but here she was, and what was she going to gain by denying it?

Mr Right had yet to come along but why not enjoy Mr Wrong? Mr Wrong would be *fun*!

'Maybe we could have a nightcap...or something...' she murmured and just like that she jumped off the side of the precipice.

Max gazed down at her averted face and clenched his hands as every dream and longing he'd ever had seemed to coalesce in this single moment.

Jesus, how could he ever have underestimated the power of desire?

He wanted to take her right here and right

now, push her against the door and do what both their bodies wanted them to do.

He might have done if there'd been the slightest chance of privacy. Instead, he curled his fingers into her hair and lowered his head and stifled a groan of absolute pleasure as his mouth covered hers. He shifted his big body against her, felt her slenderness curve into him, and a syringeful of adrenaline couldn't have had a more dramatic effect on his already soaring libido.

'We have to get out of here,' he groaned thickly, pausing only to step back an inch.

He didn't give her time to answer, instead simultaneously flipping out the key card and lifting her off her feet.

The crutch fell to the ground, but he ignored it as he carried her caveman-style into his bedroom, which was shrouded in silvery light.

He liked that, liked seeing her—liked even more the thought of seeing her with nothing on, of satisfying the curiosity that had been burning in his blood since he had first laid eyes on her.

He hadn't known how the evening was going to end. He'd *hoped*, but she was an unpredictable entity, quite unlike the women he was accustomed to. He had made sure to contain the conversation, to keep it in safe territory. Pride had dictated that he not make a blatant pass at her, but that had all gone down the drain as they'd headed to their bedrooms.

He'd been able to keep his desire at bay so far. He'd wanted to play it cool—hadn't happened.

She was on his bed, just where he'd dreamed of her being. The dress was still on, but the shoes were off, and the way she was watching him, half-shy, half-bold and plenty hungry, made him cup his hardness, controlling it through his trousers.

He breathed in deeply and half closed his eyes, hunting around for his self-control which had gone AWOL.

Then he began to undress.

Mia watched in downright fascination,

mouth parted, nostrils flared. She was so wet between her legs that she had to control an irresistible urge to touch herself, to satisfy the tickling there.

He was wearing navy boxers and her eyes were riveted to the impressive bulge distorting them.

Her breath hitched as those boxers dropped to the ground, and she shuddered and closed her eyes, parted her legs as the mattress depressed under the weight of him.

'I want you so badly,' he groaned, straddling her.

Mia could only stumble out a thick, 'Same...' and then he was reaching under the dress and tugging down her panties, and she couldn't get them off fast enough.

His mouth ravaged hers and she writhed under him, trembling, hot and aflame. He'd taken protection from his wallet, and he was fumbling to rip the foil pack open, but then he was over her once again.

Her blunt nails dug into his back as he pushed apart her legs and drove into her, fierce and deep, filling her and… *God, it felt so wonderful.*

Nothing in her life had ever warned her that her body could feel like this. Her brain shut down and she could hear herself cry out, a high, rasping sob as she came, soaring, soaring and splintering into molten hot orgasm.

Afterwards she lay still, breathing hard, utterly spent.

Her body was cool as he rolled off her, but then he manoeuvred her onto her side so that they were facing one another, belly to belly, her leg draped over his, her arm resting lightly on his waist.

It felt so natural.

'I'm sorry,' he said, and she frowned. 'You still have your dress on. I… It's not like me at all…'

He cupped her face and looked at her gravely, ruefully.

'This isn't how it was supposed to happen. You shouldn't still be wearing your dress. I just couldn't stop myself, couldn't slow down. It was all too fast, and I am truly sorry.'

'Don't be,' Mia whispered. 'It was the most wonderful thing...'

'For me too. Incredible. But next time it will be even more incredible.'

Next time... Mia loved the sound of that. Fast sex in a hotel room with a guy she wasn't in a relationship with...

All of that went against the grain. It just wasn't her, and she didn't know how cool and casual she would have been if this had turned out to be a one-night stand.

She hadn't given that a moment's thought when she had entered the bedroom with him, but now something inside her leapt at his words.

'Next time,' he delivered huskily, unsteadily, 'I'm going to go slowly...'

Mia's eyes fluttered. She had just come, her body was still warm with the afterglow of her orgasm, and yet she could feel a rising tide of desire overtaking her.

Was this how a person emerged after years of celibacy? From deep freeze to fire in the space of ten seconds?

She curled against him and he smiled, stroked her dampened hair away from her face and kissed the corner of her mouth.

In return, she trailed her hand over his chest and smiled back.

She began to prop herself up so that she could get rid of the dress but he stayed her.

'This time,' he said, sitting up, 'I'm going to pleasure you the way I should have done before. Slowly. I was selfish and it's not going to happen again. Trust me.'

He removed the dress. She leant back against the pillows and saw the flare of hunger darken his eyes as he looked at her. Never had she felt more desired. A girl could get used to this kind of thing.

She reached to unclasp her bra from behind, freeing her small breasts.

'You are beautiful,' he said in a roughened undertone. 'It's going to take every ounce of willpower to do what I'm about to do...'

'Which is?'

'I'm going to run a bath.' His voice was shaky. 'And I'm going to fill it with bubbles, and I'm going to soap you very, very gently, and then I'm going to dry you and carry you right back to this bed so that I can make love to you, taking my time.'

Every single word made her blush like a teenager transported for the first time to cloud nine by the boy of her dreams.

She let herself be pampered by him. Being naked with him like this was crazy and great at the same time and, whereas she might have quailed at the thought of walking around without her clothes on with anyone else, she found that she positively relished it.

He did as he had promised and Mia luxuriated. The bath was big enough for both of them, and sliding into the warm water with all the fragrant bubbles was heavenly.

This—all of it—felt heavenly.

Her voice was soft and relaxed as she chatted, leaning back against the white porcelain, eyes half-closed, feeling his thighs on either side of hers. The bubbles concealed their bodies, but she knew his now, and her body tingled in eager anticipation at touching him again, being touched by him.

What was going to happen in this evolving scenario? She didn't know and she didn't care.

He got out first, dried fast and roughly and told her to stay where she was. Then he ran more hot water and began to soap her at the back of her neck, massaging her shoulders, curving his big hands over her breasts.

He had wrapped a towel around his waist and he looked like a beautiful Roman emperor with his dark hair slicked back, emphasising the strong, angular lines of his remarkable face.

He beckoned for her to stand and she did, feeling exposed as the water ran off her in rivulets.

She tilted her head back, her hair damp against her back, and closed her eyes. Her skin cooled and then his soapy hands were on her, slowly working their way from her breasts, along her stomach and then parting her thighs so that he could take his time, gently soaping between her legs.

'I can't keep standing!' She gasped. 'It's too much.' Her legs had turned to jelly and she subsided back into the water...but not for long...just until he lifted her out, dried her then lifted her again and carried her over to the bed.

She was still draped in the white towel. His had slipped lower down his lean hips. He stood back and looked at her, and she smiled at him and squirmed under his scrutiny.

'Slowly this time,' he murmured, unhooking his towel and dropping it to the floor to move closer to the bed. 'This time, I'm going to explore every inch of your beautiful body.'

Max wasn't quite sure how he was going to achieve that. There she was, with that towel loosely covering her body, and he was raring to go, as horny as though he hadn't just had her. She was exquisite—so slender, so smooth—every bit of her in stunning proportion, from her small breasts to her narrow waist to the length of her legs.

He slowly removed her towel and a rush of blood fired up inside him with the immediacy of a conflagration. She was incredibly delicate, but so well-toned from the amount of physical exercise she got from just her daily activities.

He joined her on the bed, trailed his finger across her cheek and then along her collarbone and enjoyed the way she trembled, sighed and quivered. He found the tip of her brown nipple and teased it in ever-decreasing circles until it was stiff and throbbing. In response, she covered her face with her arm, but he could see her mouth half open with pleasure.

It took willpower he'd never known he had to resist the urge to go hot, hard and fast. Instead, he lowered to take one throbbing nipple in his mouth, and she moaned as his questing mouth suckled and teased.

His big body tensed and then relaxed when she stroked his shoulder lightly, curling up to caress his ear and the side of his jawline.

Her legs were open for him. He could feel

her knees pressed against his thighs, inviting him, and he couldn't resist. But still he took his time, inching down her stomach with his tongue to circle her belly button and jab delicately into the small indent, while the rhythm of her body told him just how much she was enjoying this.

He planned on her enjoying it even more. He was going to take her to paradise and back, and it felt very, very important that he do that…that he show her just how much he could pleasure her, how much they could enjoy one another. Nothing had ever seemed more vital.

She weakly tried to clamp her legs together as he nudged his way there, but he gently, firmly parted her thighs, a hand on the soft inner flesh of either one, and darted his tongue along the slippery groove of her womanhood, sheathed in soft, downy pubic hair.

He probed the delicate folds with his tongue to find the pulsing nub of her clitoris and he settled down between her legs, teasing that sensitive place while she squirmed against him, pushing towards his mouth and pulling away, coming so close to the edge and then backing off.

He wasn't going to let her come against his mouth, but he couldn't hold off much longer.

He raised himself, breathing hard, and for a few moments just rubbed his aroused hardness against her silky wetness, only breaking off to protect himself and relishing the few seconds it gave him to try and contain his wild response.

This time round, he came into her slowly, easing himself in and feeling her tightness around him with a groan of pure pleasure. When he kissed her, it was with great tenderness. He kissed her mouth, her eyes, the soft flesh of her cheek. He waited for her to be just ready for him to take her to that place and, when she was...when she urged him on, face flushed and her body burning up with wanting...then and only then did he thrust deep and hard, taking them both to a shuddering orgasm.

He'd never felt anything like it.

Utterly spent, he lay on her for a while.

'I'm too heavy for you.'

You're perfect for me... Mia thought.

He rolled off onto his side and then pulled her in against him.

'Was that as amazing for you as it was for me?' he asked softly, and she smiled.

'Better. Better than amazing. After my marriage broke up, I guess I hid away from relationships. At first, I was just grieving the loss of my marriage, but then after a while… I suppose I just found that I wasn't interested.'

'You must have had guys asking you out?'

'When I thought about dating again, my mind went blank. It became a habit to be on my own. I enjoyed it.'

'Everything becomes a habit after a while.' He stroked her hair from her face.

'What's become a habit for you?'

Max hesitated. Out here, being with this woman, was like being in a temporary bubble and, from within it, his life back in London seemed gilded but jaded. Was that because work had become a habit? He shifted uncomfortably at the thought of that because he was defined by work. Where would he be if it became no more than something that filled the days? Something he had grown accustomed to, without any merit of its own?

Of course, he had women, but if *her* habit had become avoiding the business of dating, then surely his was avoiding the business of dating for longer than two months?

'There's a certain tedium attached to the business of making money,' he eventually murmured.

'But you don't have to do it, do you? Surely you have enough?'

He grinned at her. 'You'd think.' He frowned. 'It's not so much the business of having cash in a bank account. If it were simply a matter of money per se, then you're right. I have enough. It's the enjoyment of how that cash gets made that's addictive.' He grinned again at her silent scepticism. 'And maybe...' he added thoughtfully.

'Maybe what?'

'And maybe...' His voice lightened. 'We should grab some sleep. I have a packed itinerary for tomorrow and the crutch will have to be left behind. I'll carry you if needs be.'

Maybe the habit of having to make money because his siblings depended on it had become too ingrained to break, but really, was there any need to drive himself for the sake of James and Izzy? He'd done his bit. James, certainly, was incredibly successful in his own right, contributing to the family empire while also running his own highly profitable computer software businesses, and Izzy was clearly a big girl now, even if he hadn't seen it coming.

So what was with the pressure to keep earning?

And what did he think would happen if he kicked back?

Would he have to re-evaluate his priorities? He dismissed any such thought with consummate ease.

Mia kissed his chin. There were times, few

and far between when something happened between them, when she glimpsed a vulnerability inside him that roused feelings in her, far removed from sexual feelings, that were oddly tender.

He'd confided in her, but then he'd stopped, and she wasn't going to press him to tell her anything he didn't want to.

He was proud and he was arrogant but not because he set out to be that way. That was simply the way he *was*, nothing to do with trying to impress or instil fear. She loathed all forms of arrogance but she'd come to see that, with Max, it was a trait that was intensely appealing, and very, very sexy, because it was so utterly unconscious.

She began to sit up, scouting around for the dress and her underwear.

'Where do you think you're off to?' he drawled lazily, running his finger along her spine and then tugging her back so that she fell against him, laughing.

'Off to my room,' Mia told him, wriggling so that she could look at him.

'No way.'

'What do you mean?'

'I might want you in the middle of the night, and then what am I supposed to do if you're not in my bed?'

Mia laughed. Inside, she was thrilled—*too* thrilled. She wanted to keep reminding herself that this was a fling and nothing more, no castles in the air waiting to be built.

She opened her mouth to remind him that he was her boss, and if they had temporarily suspended common sense then that didn't change the reality of the situation, but she didn't go there. She knew, almost immediately, that she didn't want that untimely reminder to spoil anything.

She'd just had the most incredible experience of her life. Why would she want to give him the wherewithal to end it? Like a thief in the night, she wanted to grab whatever more there was to come, steal those experiences so that she could hoard them inside her for the rest of her life.

On the other hand, there was such a thing as pride.

'Who says I would want to be awakened at some ungodly hour in the morning to… to…?'

'To make sweet, passionate and unforgettable love with me?' He kissed her, a long, slow-burning kiss that had her weak with wanting more.

'I'm not used to sharing a bed with anyone,' she said truthfully, and he drew back to look at her seriously.

'Nor am I.' He kissed her eyes and the side of her mouth, tugging her hair so that he could feather more kisses along the slender column of her neck. 'But there are such things as exceptions to rules…'

'There are, I guess.' She tried but how was she supposed to resist what he was doing to her? His words were as seductive as melting honey. Wading through them to get to the cautious, sensible person she was at the other side seemed an impossible mission.

She sank back in his arms and allowed herself to be thoroughly kissed.

And sleep that night?

Very broken. She was so conscious of the weight of him next to her. In the darkness, she could make out his outline, one leg splayed across the cool cotton sheets and his arm across her nakedness even when he'd fallen asleep.

At some point she too must have fallen asleep, because she was roused, slowly and sensuously, by the nudge of his swollen girth against her, finding her building wetness.

'You said,' he murmured with laughter in his voice, 'that you might object to being awakened at an ungodly hour in the morning by me...'

'Did I?' She curved against him and reached down to feather her finger along his throbbing penis. He was rock-solid. She could feel the veins of his shaft and he inhaled sharply when she teased the tip of it with her thumb in small, circular movements. 'I can't remember that at all.'

She felt his rumble of laughter. If he could tease her beyond sanity, then she could tease him as well, and the silent darkness was a comforting blanket, squashing any vague notions of shyness she might have felt.

She manoeuvred herself with dexterity until she could administer to him with her tongue and her mouth. She had never been this intimate with a man before and it was a slow, sweet process of discovery.

As she licked and teased with her tongue, as she folded her lips over him and gently sucked, she was finding out that he was as weak as she was when it came to resisting the build-up of desire.

She had absolute control here, in this bed, in the darkness of the night, over this big, invincible, self-assured male, and she loved the feeling.

She gasped when he hoisted her gently so that he could do to her exactly what she was doing to him.

His face buried between her thighs and the dart of his tongue sent her pulses racing, deprived her of breath, and they pleasured one another for as long as they could before it wasn't enough.

Their lovemaking was fast and hard and she came on a sob of wrenching abandon, shuddering as her orgasm brought tears to her eyes.

How could she ever have thought that sleeping on her own in a cold bed could be better than this? And how had she never been curious about the joy of sex when you were still warm from the languor of sleep?

'Time for sleep,' he mock-ordered in a soft, amused voice when their breathing had finally returned to normal. 'We have a packed agenda tomorrow. I can't have you waking me up all the time to satisfy your needs.'

Mia giggled and mentally added 'funny' to the list she was compiling in her head. Where had that one-dimensional guy gone? The one she had written off as a workaholic with not much else going for him? Every second she was in his company revealed more and more complex and fascinating sides to him.

She certainly didn't wake him, at least not for the remainder of the night, although she couldn't resist reaching out when, at a little after six the following morning, she woke to his warmth next to her on the bed, so close, breathing deep and even, begging to be touched.

She greedily stole a long, satisfied look at his beautiful face, drinking in the strong lines, so much less forbidding in repose. He had the most amazing lashes. Long and thick and dark.

Then she touched him, touched and settled her hand around his shaft, keeping it there as he opened his eyes and looked at her.

No words were spoken. Some time during the night—or maybe in the early hours of the morning…she didn't know when—he had obviously switched off the air-conditioning and chosen to use the overhead fan instead. Now, the faint whirr of the blades was the only sound in the bedroom.

That and their breathing.

Eyes locked, she pushed clear the sheets and continued slowly to massage him, ever so gently, but firmly building a rhythm, watching with mounting desire as she began taking him to the edge. His groans were deep and unsteady and his fingers curled into the sheet.

He erupted in her hand with a long moan of satisfaction. She felt his hot liquid running over her flesh and nothing, she swore, had ever felt better.

'Wicked.' His navy eyes glinted and he pulled her down to him. 'But very, *very* nice.'

'Happy to be of service,' Mia said, kissing him and sliding one leg over his so that she could ease the urgent ache between her thighs.

And lovemaking, as she soon found out, was not one-sided with him.

He took her to the same heights she had taken him, and afterwards she was so pleasantly content that she could have fallen asleep again.

'Shame we have to work,' she said, drowsy

and flushed in the aftermath of their morning lovemaking, and he smiled a long, slow smile.

'Work? I don't think so. For once in my life...' His tone was oddly quizzical. 'I think I'm going to take some well-deserved time out...'

CHAPTER NINE

TIME OUT WAS…a holiday.

Max hadn't been kidding when he'd told Mia that time out was a once-in-a-lifetime experience for him. When was the last time he'd jettisoned work in favour of relaxation?

They spent three nights in Maui. They were driven to local beauty spots as Mia's foot healed. There was over one hundred and twenty miles of coastline and over thirty miles of beach. They went to South Maui and sat with an elaborate picnic at one of the tables at Makena Beach, watching the people and the activity, and the deep turquoise sea and the billowing clouds, blowing fast in a blue sky.

She was discovering just how the world of the truly rich worked and it was nothing like anything she'd seen in her life before. People jumped at his command. After their first night together, the following day he had announced that he wouldn't countenance her sleeping separately from him.

'We could…er…get the hotel to unlock the adjoining door,' Mia had suggested.

He was used to obedience. He spoke, people listened and then they duly did as they were told.

She could understand how Izzy had fallen into line with all the laws and regulations he had laid down over the years.

She wasn't his sister, however, and, although she was his employee, they were now on a different standing, in a different place, and she was not going to succumb to the overwhelming power of his personality.

At least, she certainly wasn't going to join the troupe of *yes, sir* people who surrounded him.

She fought to stick to sleeping apart but an open door between their suites had been a recipe for a very disrupted second night.

He'd come to her bed and scooped her up,

had carried her to his, and then had duly delivered her right back to her own bed. But she missed him. If he wanted to have her right there at hand, then it was a two-way street, because she wanted the same thing.

By night three, all notion of sleeping apart had duly been abandoned.

'You're very bossy,' she'd told him at one point, and he'd burst out laughing.

'I have no idea what you're talking about. No one's ever called me *bossy* before.'

'That's because they're all scared of you,' Mia had retorted without blinking an eye, which had resulted in yet more mirth.

'Everyone but you,' he had said softly.

'When you come from a large, noisy family, it doesn't pay to be shy and retiring.'

But she was uneasily aware that the power of his personality and his assumption that he called the shots was an almost irresistible force and, quite often, she just relished basking in his alpha male strength.

They left Maui on the very same private

jet that had delivered them there, flying in to Kauai.

He'd booked yet another luxury five-star hotel.

Now, as the jet disgorged them into brilliant sun, and humidity that made her clothes instantly stick to her back like glue, Mia tilted her head up to look at him.

He took her breath away. Especially now that her thoughts were no longer forbidden. She was *allowed* to admire him; she was *allowed* to appreciate his superb masculine beauty. The very slight breeze ruffled his dark hair, which was longer now, and her breath caught in her throat. He was in a white polo shirt and a pair of light grey shorts that just about hit his knees and loafers, and he looked every inch pure sex on legs. His fingers linked through hers was a vibrant reminder of the bond they now shared.

Over the past few days, he had expanded his wardrobe. The prospect of actually going to one of the many designer outlets and trying anything on had clearly bored him to death so he had simply snapped his fingers and got someone to do the leg work, returning with everything he'd asked for. He'd simply glanced at what had been bought, nodded and got someone else carefully to put them away.

'You're so spoiled,' Mia had said, although his complete expectation that he could be spared all manner of what he called 'dreary, non-profitable nonsense I can't be bothered with' was somehow incredibly appealing and very amusing.

'Why do what other people can do better?' he had countered. 'I'm a lousy cook, so I have a personal chef, and I dislike shopping so I get someone else to do it for me. Seems to make perfect sense, as far as I'm concerned.'

'This hotel we're booked in,' Mia said now, as they were escorted from the opulent confines of the jet to a similar level of opulence in a shiny black Range Rover.

'Yes?' Once inside the car, he turned to her and raised his eyebrows. 'I'm beginning to recognise a certain tone of voice. It usually warns me that your school mistress hat is about to be donned…'

'No idea what you're talking about,' Mia sniffed, and he grinned.

'Have I ever told you you're very sexy when you're wearing that particular hat?'

'I admit I *am* about to offer a suggestion which you may or may not like…'

'Would I need a stiff drink to deal with what's coming?'

Mia looked at him but trying to maintain any hauteur was out of the question when she saw the warm, teasing glint in his eyes.

Had she ever felt this comfortable with any guy in her life before? Even Kai?

'It's fine staying in posh hotels, but you know Izzy had something else in mind for your hotel. In fact, there's a hotel she specifically visited this island to stay on. She was so enthusiastic about it afterwards. Showed me photos. Well, I think it would be a nice idea for us to go stay there. I know it might be a bit inconvenient, because you've booked this place we're heading to for a couple of nights, but...'

'I could go with that,' Max said thoughtfully.

'Really?'

'Really,' he said, voice wry. 'Why the doubts in the first place?'

'You like your comforts.'

'Who doesn't? Mia, answer me truthfully. Would you rather be in this car or standing in a queue waiting for a bus to trundle along, in soaring heat and insane humidity.'

'I never minded before,' she said stoutly. 'I happen to be very accustomed to taking public transport to get everywhere. Or cycling. In soaring heat and insane humidity.'

'But, my darling, that was before you met me.' His voice was low and lazy and teasing.

Mia shivered.

Had she changed? Had she grown used to his world? No, she was still the same girl she'd always been, even if this girl was now moving in a different world. What had changed was that this girl now had fun. He could make her laugh the way no one else could and every second in his company thrilled, challenged and excited her. But what was going to happen when she packed her bags and left that world behind?

He had said that this was time out for him, and he hadn't been lying. Work had been left behind in Oahu. He touched base with his sprawling empire for a couple of hours, often in the early hours of the morning. They didn't talk about the hotel or any of the myriad things that needed doing.

What had started as a four-day trip had very quickly blossomed into a ten-day plan.

'I can do whatever I want.' He had shrugged when she had asked him about that. 'Working all the hours God made does confer certain advantages. Freedom of movement is one of them.'

She'd been guiltily thrilled at that, but time was moving on and was she digging a hole for herself by settling into this uber-lavish life he had handed her on a plate? Shouldn't she be remembering that there was no such thing as a free lunch and that, when the time came to say goodbye to all of this, she might just find it harder than she could ever have imagined?

Shouldn't she be remembering that when the time came to say goodbye to him she might just find it impossible?

They had fun. The lovemaking was intense and extraordinary. They seemed to physically fit one another like a hand in a glove. They talked and laughed but no mention was ever made of anything beyond the moment. He had no expectations that what they had was going to last. When he spoke about returning to London, she was noticeably absent from any of the scenarios.

She had talked herself into taking what was on offer, because she deserved to have a bit of fun in her life for once, but had she bitten off more than she could chew?

He was a man of the world, experienced when it came to picking up women, enjoying them and then moving on without a backward glance.

She was wet behind the ears in comparison.

'I'm the same person I always was,' she said now. 'I haven't changed.'

'No?'

'Have you?' She turned the question to him. Suddenly, it felt very constricted in the back of the car. He looked at her through narrowed eyes and she flushed, wondering whether he could read what was going through her head.

'Not getting where you're going with that question,' he drawled, and the teasing warmth she had grown accustomed to was absent.

Suddenly, she wanted nothing more than for this sudden tense atmosphere to go away. What was the point in trying to find out whether there was more to what they had than this? Gut feeling told her what would happen if she pressed the point. He would walk away. She knew it.

With sudden clarity, she recognised what she had wilfully been hiding from herself. She had developed feelings for him. Strong feelings. Feelings that went way beyond lust, desire and all those other convenient descriptions she'd been using.

Lust and desire were passing viruses. Once she'd established that with herself, she'd had no trouble reasoning with herself that she was in no danger of being hurt. But now...

His fabulous eyes were on her face, incisive, penetrating and looking for...something she had no intention of revealing.

'You don't work as much as you used to,' she said, deflecting his question. 'Do you think you'll slow down when you get back to London?'

'Not a chance of it,' he murmured, dropping his eyes, his long, lush lashes shielding his expression for a few seconds before he looked at her once again. 'This is a holiday, but holidays don't last for ever...'

'You're so right.' She smiled while something inside twisted painfully, because if this wasn't telling her like it was, just in case she started getting ideas, then what was? 'The reason I asked is... I'll be very happy indeed to go back to my usual life. I miss my surfing and, believe it or not, all this luxury travel is terrible for a girl's figure!'

'How so?'

'Not enough exercise and too much fine dining. I shall end up the size of one of those humpbacked whales in Maui if I'm not careful! Also, I just thought about my backlog of work. Neither of us has been up to speed with work-related issues.' *Work-related issues?* She sounded like a business manual!

'I'm assuming there won't be a lot of fine dining when we shift location to whatever resort you have in mind?'

Mia began to relax. Somehow, they'd skirted around what had suddenly felt like a contentious issue, and she was pleased to be back in known territory.

Except…something had been added to the mix and she would be an idiot not to pay heed. He'd reminded her that all good things would have to come to an end.

'And as for your other work,' he said, 'I don't think taking a breather for a few days is going to cause any insoluble problems with whatever work you might have on at the moment, will it?'

Mia frowned and thought about a couple of her outstanding projects. She had been in touch with the clients, explained the situation, and had emailed them various landscaping ideas. It would take time to order in just the right plants anyway, and they had been happy to wait until her return.

That said, pride clamped firmly round her fragile heart, stiffening her backbone. If he could issue his opportune reminders, then surely she could respond in kind?

'I'll set aside some time later to deal with any outstanding issues,' she murmured.

'And let me know if you run into any roadblocks…'

'Why would I do that?' she asked, surprised.

'I'm extremely good at sorting out road blocks, my darling.' He sent her a slow, curling smile that made her shiver and sent a shot of hot adrenaline racing through her bloodstream.

From tension to blistering excitement in the

space of five minutes. Was it any wonder she had landed herself in more hot water than she could ever have imagined? She wasn't adapted for an emotional life lived in the fast lane.

'Really?' she murmured, keeping her cool and giving no inkling to her tumultuous emotions. 'And how would you solve those sorts of roadblocks?'

'I'd get whoever was kicking up a fuss to get in touch with me.'

'Now you sound like someone from the Mafia.' But her eyes were glinting with helpless amusement.

Max laughed, his gaze resting on her face, looking at her as though she were the only person on the planet. 'Nothing so dramatic,' he drawled, feathering his finger on the inside of her wrist and setting up a ferocious fire trail of response inside her. 'Or dangerous. I would merely give them enough money to persuade them that I need my woman by me for a few uninterrupted days.'

His woman. Giddy thought. Also foolish,

because she wasn't his woman…she was his passing interest. 'A few uninterrupted days' said it all.

'Well,' she said crisply, 'I'm sure it won't come to that. I have very understanding clients, and in Honolulu people are patient when it comes to getting work done.' She paused and looked at him seriously. 'But if I *do* encounter any problems—' she grinned, lightening her tone '—I'll make sure *not* to tell you! The last thing I'd want is for any of them to be scared away by a Big Bad Wolf!'

She looked ahead as the car slowed and realised that they were here. Destination reached before the conversation could go down any more tricky roads. 'Looks amazing.' She directed her dancing eyes at him. 'Make sure you lap up the luxury. You never know where I'm going to take you tomorrow!'

Max gazed at the ocean in front of them. It was after six. Behind them, nestled in swaying trees, was a beast of a motorbike that he had rented a couple of days ago so that they could tour the island and get to all the places that Mia had told him in no uncertain terms he needed to see if he were to fully understand his sister's vision for the hotel.

He hadn't ridden a motorbike since his university days. Along with his vague plans to see something of the world before settling down and joining the rat race, motorbikes had been ditched when his parents had died and he'd had his wake-up call.

Along from the trees, via a network of winding paths through coconut palm trees and giant firs, was the eco-hotel where they were now staying.

When he'd first seen it, he'd thought they'd made a mistake and landed up at someone's house. A triangular children's drawing of what a house should look like, with a red roof and weathered turquoise walls and wide shallow steps leading up to a heavy wooden door. Around them, there must be a million different types of tree and bush and flower and fern, all pressing against the open clearing around the hotel, for hotel it was, as he soon discovered once they were inside.

There was an air of casual professionalism about the place. The floorboards shone and there were plants everywhere. There was no air-conditioning, which they considered a threat to the planet, but instead overhead fans. It was tiny in comparison to the places he was accustomed to, and although clearly busy it felt uncrowded, with everyone having their own space, and most people out exploring the great outdoors.

A constant breeze blew through all the many open windows and the dining was informal, with a choice of individual square white tables or else a long, gleaming communal table for anyone wanting to socialise with other guests and listen in to the various speakers they had on a twice-weekly basis.

It was out of his comfort zone, but then what wasn't ever since he had landed in Hawaii?

He gazed down at the woman lying curled into him. The silence between them was comfortable, peaceful. They'd biked straight here from the lush waterfalls they had visited earlier. They were tired but still too wired to head into the hotel.

'Fancy a dip?' She turned to him and he frowned.

'What, now?' He looked out to the ocean which was black, streaked with silver from the full moon.

'Sure.' She sprang to her feet, lithe and supple and sandy and utterly bewitching.

'No chance.'

'You're not scared, are you?' she teased. 'You don't have to worry. I'm an expert swimmer. I'm used to the sea, in the daytime and at night.'

'You've done this before?' Max asked gruffly.

'Of course, I have! Lots of times. Don't forget, this is my home. I grew up with the ocean all around me. I don't scare easily when it comes to the sea.'

She was already stepping out of the small denim shorts she was wearing, reaching to strip off the cropped white tee shirt. Her hair was all over the place, half over her eyes as she looked down at him, laughing.

And he looked right back at her, and all he could see was a vision of her being consumed by the deep, black ocean. The rush of protectiveness that attacked him was so fierce that for a few seconds he couldn't breathe.

His heart was hammering and he had all the symptoms of a man in full panic attack mode.

He wanted to leap to his feet, hold her tight and keep holding her. He wanted to keep holding her until she was persuaded never to enter the water again at night, never even to contemplate the idea, never, indeed, to stray far from his possessive gaze.

What the hell was going on?

This was what his parents had all been about, he thought, as the reality he had kept at bay now slammed into him with the force of a freight train.

Hadn't he seen the havoc emotion could cause? Hadn't he been a casualty of their all-consuming love? They had abandoned restraint in the name of love and he—all of them—had paid the price.

He had sworn from an early age to exercise control over his life, but here he was now, worrying over a woman who hadn't even done anything yet. Worrying at the thought of her swimming in that dark ocean, prey to currents, eddies and whatever dodgy sea creatures might be lurking just below the surface.

It was an alien experience and he didn't like it. It made him edgy and unsettled.

His original plan for a flying visit to a country he'd had no interest in seeing had been scuppered at the starting block. Instead of reining in the situation, he had found himself going along for the ride, curious to see where it would lead.

What did they say about curiosity killing cats?

He had allowed lust to dictate the pace of a relationship with a woman who worked for him. Yes, the situation was an unusual one, but she was still his employee, and he had always had very clear ideas about having any sort of physical relationship with someone who worked for him.

And yet, he had fallen into bed with Mia with only the merest of reservations.

He'd managed to persuade himself that this was a different life. Somehow. He'd successfully managed to convince himself that this was a much-deserved holiday, under which banner it had been okay to push aside all dissenting inner voices.

He'd slept with her and she'd stayed in his bed and he'd wanted her there. Sleeping next to him, warm and responsive to his touch, always there when he wanted her.

And this four-day trek across the islands? He'd sensibly written that off as an important way of getting to grips with what his sister had been after when it came to the hotel. Sure, by then, he'd also seen it as a good way of having Mia to himself, of indulging a need that had tailgated him from behind and thrown him off course when he had least been expecting it.

Everything neatly wrapped up as acceptable because he deserved a holiday...deserved some time out...

Roll the clock on, and here he was, worrying about her, looking at her and imagining all sorts of nonsense, his stomach clenched into a tight knot.

He felt as though he had hit some kind of crossroads.

Where did he think this was going to go? he asked himself. They lived in different countries. He had to return to London. He couldn't put his life on hold indefinitely and there was no way he was going to contemplate the unthinkable—there was *no way* he would contemplate asking her to return with him. He didn't want a woman in his life on any sort of semi-permanent basis. Never had, never would. They'd shared a handful of days together...but he would never allow himself to get so wrapped up with any woman that he couldn't consider a life without her.

Mia couldn't quite make out the expression on his face but, with a sort of sixth sense she seemed to have developed when it came to him, she *knew* that something was wrong.

What?

'It…it was just a thought,' she stammered. 'I mean, the business of going for a swim…'

Scrambling to try and work out what was going on, she chanced a smile and held out her hand to him, desperately wanting to feel the warmth on which she had become dependent.

He stood up and when he didn't take her hand she let hers drop to her side. A coldness was spreading through her.

'I didn't tell you,' he drawled. 'I heard from Izzy.'

'What? When?' She was swamped with relief because it must be whatever conversation he'd had with Izzy that had thrown him off-balance. Had he been waiting to talk to her about it once their hectic day came to a close?

'Pretty much as soon as we got back here.' He began walking towards the hotel, leaving the motorbike where it was, only glancing at it in passing. He would ask someone to ride it to the courtyard and secure it. His hands were shoved into his pockets and she hesitated to take one because something didn't feel right.

The hotel was brightly lit, the trees rustling in the breeze and shadows cast by the moonlight. The air was cooler but still balmy, still humid.

'Are you going to tell me what she said? Is she okay?'

'She won't be returning just yet.' He carried on walking straight through the foyer, where several guests turned to them and smiled. In a small hotel, you quickly got to know who your fellow travellers were.

They were heading straight up to their bedroom suite. It was an expansive space with billowing voile curtains, a mosquito net draped over a super-king-sized bed, an overhead fan and lots of bamboo furniture that complemented the rich patina of wood everywhere.

'It's time we had a talk,' he said, as soon as the door was shut behind them, and the coldness she had felt earlier returned with force. But she held on to her composure, because surely she'd known that this moment would come, sooner or later?

'Has she said why?' Mia sat on a rocking chair by the window, but then leaned forward, tense with nerves.

'She's…somehow got herself involved with trying to save my mother's nanny from being evicted from her house. Long story short, she decamped to my mother's house in California. Should have put two and two together and worked that out for myself but…' He shrugged. 'She'll be back, and I'm willing for her to have a revised role when it comes to the hotel.'

Mia hadn't heard from her friend for a while and she breathed a sigh of relief that everything was okay. She wasn't surprised that Izzy had adopted a noble cause. She had a tender heart and a hugely caring disposition.

'That's all good, then, isn't it? It must have been awesome talking to her, having her call you.'

'At any rate, if you recall I had begun the process of auditioning for someone to take over the financial side of the operation...'

'I know you said that Nat's interviewed a few candidates.'

'He has but I was holding off for my sister's decision one way or another. That decision has been made and an offer has been tendered to a highly respected chartered accountant with a background in the leisure industry. He should find the process of dealing with all the various supply chains easy to manoeuvre.'

Mia nodded but she was wondering where this was going and why she had such a bad feeling about the direction of the conversation. Was it the flat coolness in his eyes? Or was she imagining that?

'So,' he went on, 'you could say that my time here is officially at an end.' He lowered his eyes and then looked at her without expression.

Mia's heart slowed down. This was how it had always been going to end. Not with a bang, but a whimper. No great fireworks, no storming off after a heated argument, no revelations and tears. Just a quiet ending to something that always had a timeline attached to it. It was up to her to deal with it because she had gone into this with her eyes wide open.

'Well…' She floundered, trying hard to contain the burst dam through which her emotions were pouring. 'It's great that everything's been settled.' She smiled ruefully. 'And you're right. All good things come to an end.'

'And this has been good. Really good.' Rueful smile for rueful smile.

There was a heartbeat of a pause, then Mia resumed the conversation. She was frozen to the spot, and breaking up inside, but thankfully her voice was steady.

'Yes, it has been,' she said politely. 'And I should thank you.'

'For what?'

'For…' She sighed and meant every word when she said, 'For getting me out of my hibernation. I've said this before to you—the failure of my marriage affected me a whole lot more than I could ever have anticipated. I went into hiding, and then you came along and you led me out, and I will always be grateful to you for that.'

'Grateful…' Max murmured.

'You've done me a huge favour,' she said brightly.

'And you could do me a huge favour now,' he growled with an edge of harshness to his voice that she just didn't get. Because what the heck did he have to be annoyed about? Wasn't he about to head back to his high-powered life with its sophisticated women? Back to what he knew? He probably couldn't wait. She'd done her bit and now he'd probably had his fill of down time for the next five years. Leopards never changed their spots.

'How so?'

'By coming here.' He didn't give her time to answer. He moved towards her and cupped the nape of her neck and drew her towards him. Their bodies were still sticky from the heat and the humidity. He kissed her. Long and hard and with a hunger that was like nothing she'd felt with him before.

He propelled her back towards the bed, holding her so tightly that it was very nearly painful.

And then everything in a rush. Clothes shed... His hand on her breasts, her thighs, between them... Just time to fumble for protection but barely breaking away from his devouring embrace...

He lifted her off her feet and she wrapped her legs around him, felt the powerful thrust of his erection hard inside her as he backed them towards the wall.

She heard herself cry out on a guttural sob of release, a long shudder tearing through her, and afterwards she clung on. Just for a while. Just for her time to say goodbye in that embrace. Tears would come later.

CHAPTER TEN

MAX STARED OUT into an impenetrable night. Two weeks. Two weeks, three days and he could probably count the hours if he put his mind to it.

In short, a lifetime since he had boarded that plane back to London, and back to his precious comfort zone, without which he had been convinced he could not live. Life was work. Work allowed him the control he craved. He knew where he was in the complex, cut-throat world of making money and he liked knowing where he was.

That was what he had told himself when he had left Hawaii, and he had kept feeding himself the same lines, over and over and over.

Izzy was still away, playing Good Samaritan to their mother's elderly nanny and friend. They had now spoken several times and a cool layer of ice he had not really known existed was rapidly thawing. He had gone to Hawaii to drag his sister out from wherever she was hiding, to find out what the hell she thought she was playing at and to return to London, mission accomplished, within the week.

Instead, his life had been turned on its head.

He now had more insight into his sister than he had ever had before. She would be returning, but with a new, creative role and his absolute trust that she would do a fantastic job taking the hotel down a completely different direction from the one he had originally had in mind.

The new accountant was settling in with flying colours. He'd had frequent communications from Nat, in which details were given of each and every aspect of the hotel in laborious detail.

And Mia...?

Nothing. Not a word. Zilch.

He had walked away and she had cheerfully waved him off. That last night on the island, in that special bubble that had been about to burst, had been incredible. If something inside him had been strangely painful, he had successfully managed to sweep the feeling under the carpet, because he had already begun his mantra on the importance of returning to real life.

Besides, he could remember thinking, it wasn't as if *she* had kicked up a fuss that what they had shared was coming to an end. She had shrugged and smiled and been philosophical, and had behaved in exactly the way he should have been cheering about. Instead, he had been inexplicably disgruntled by her nonchalance.

But that too he had swept under the carpet, consigned, he'd thought, to oblivion, with his comfort zone back in London already within striking distance.

Of course, he would miss her. She had occupied a unique place in his life. For the first time, he had dared to stop being the man the rest of the world feared. He had dropped the shutters safe in the knowledge that it was a temporary situation, no harm done.

But now, here he was, staring through the windows of his multi-million-pound penthouse. Finally, he had to admit in the still of the night what he had known all along.

He missed her.

He thought about her all the time. He could barely focus on his work.

He remembered everything about her, from her smile and her laughter to the way she could prise information out of him so that it had always felt good to confide.

He remembered the way she felt and moved and curved against him, and the feeling that they had somehow *belonged* together.

But for all that, when the crunch had come, the barriers had been raised and he had pushed her away. Why? Because he had been scared. He had remembered his parents and the way their love had been so all-consuming that everything and everyone had been filtered out. Poor decisions had been made, responsibilities abandoned.

The second he had felt the shift of quicksand underneath his feet, he had responded with knee-jerk speed. No way had he been going to let someone get under his skin. That could only spell disaster.

He'd been a coward. He hadn't been man enough to admit to himself that he'd fallen in love with her, but subconsciously he had recognised those feelings, and had reacted by running away because to love was to love control of your life.

It had been safer to escape.

Fact was, he had fallen in love with Mia almost from the start. He'd told her that she was refreshing, but not once had he stopped to consider how much he adored that, how little he'd minded her consistently trampling over the barriers.

At every turn he had made excuses for feelings that had grown and grown until he had been forced to confront them on that last day together.

Izzy's decision to stay on in California was the catalyst he had used to propel him back to London. His time in Hawaii was at an end and he had to return to his wonderful life in London—which, he'd discovered, wasn't worth living because the one person he wanted in it was thousands of miles away.

Thing was...did she love *him?*

She did. Didn't she? So much tenderness... And when she'd looked at him...

He'd never asked, never implied that he felt anything for her at all except lust. He'd promised nothing and had reminded her on more than one occasion that what they were having was a holiday fling. He'd encouraged her at every turn to look forward to walking away, even if he hadn't always come right out and said so, because he would return to London and that would be the end of them.

He'd been a fool, but even fools deserved second chances. They at least had to try and get them.

He finished his drink and it took less than an hour for arrangements to be made to take him back to Hawaii.

He'd surprised her once. He would surprise her again.

* * *

The sun was fading but it was still very hot. Mia could feel the stirrings of a headache. Nothing new there. For the past two and a half weeks, she had felt under the weather, as though somehow all the energy had been sucked out of her and, just like that, she'd deflated. A slowly leaking balloon, lifeless and drifting on the wind.

Out here, the beach was packed with people. Tourists, locals, old, young, fat, thin—all out enjoying the sun and the sea and the surf. She could smell all different kinds of food in the air, their aromas blending and mixing and vibrant. Music was playing. The kids she had just finished teaching were babbling and laughing, and she knew that she was going through all the right motions but her heart wasn't in it.

Her heart had been left behind on another island, broken up into pieces when Max had calmly told her that what they had was over. Things had been settled with the hotel in Hawaii and there was no longer a reason for him to remain.

She'd smiled and smiled and smiled, and told herself that she should have been braced for this, because it was always going to end, and it wasn't as though she hadn't had ample warnings. They'd made love, had breakfast together and carried on talking, both adults, cool and composed—but for her every minute spent in his company had been a shard of glass piercing her heart.

Somewhere deep inside she wished she'd had the courage to say what she was thinking, to tell him how she felt, but in the end what would have been the point?

She would have to carry on with her life, just as she'd carried on with her life after her marriage had crashed and burned. Only with Max…

She could never have foreseen how deeply she would fall in love with him. Nothing had prepared her for that because he was so unlike the kind of guy she had ever imagined herself falling for.

Just went to show—life had a nasty habit of throwing curve balls.

She was a million miles away when she knew, *sensed,* that someone was behind her.

The hairs on the back of her neck stood on end but she kept on walking away from the beach and back towards her bicycle, a good ten-minute walk away.

She only felt a tug of apprehension when she realised that whoever was following her was speeding up, moving alongside her, ignoring the fact that she was walking fast, eyes down, body language rejecting any attempts at conversation.

Her fists were clenched, and she wasn't expecting it when suddenly someone's hand was on her arm.

She swung round, absolutely enraged that anyone would *dare* lay a hand on her, try to stop her. Basically, that was called assault, and in her frame of mind, with all the unhappiness and misery pent up inside her, she was ready to punch.

She raised her eyes and stopped dead in

her tracks and her mouth dropped open and she stared at the last person she had ever expected to see.

He'd accosted her once before on this very beach and she had to blink to make sure her eyes weren't deceiving her.

They weren't. He was standing right there in front of her, his back to the sun and as tall, dark and gloriously, sinfully handsome as she remembered.

She recognised the grey-and-white-striped polo shirt. She recognised the slim, grey Bermuda shorts that accentuated the muscular length of his legs. She recognised the loafers. He'd worn them on the last day they'd spent together, when his bags had been packed and he'd been ready to go.

Most of all...oh...how she recognised the depth of those navy eyes, the curve of his sensual mouth, the proud symmetry of his beautiful face.

'Max!' Something must have happened with the hotel. She'd limited her time there to working furiously on the acreage, having sections cleared for the plants on order so that everything would be ready and waiting when the time came. She hadn't been near the hotel at all, although she knew that it was coming along in leaps and bounds now that Izzy's original designs had been approved.

Had he been unable to locate Nat? She assumed he needed to know something about her end of things.

All of this raced through her head in seconds, overriding the simple question: couldn't he just have emailed her if he had something to ask?

In her head, she frantically joined the dots… *Max, here, work.* She should smile. She shouldn't let him see that the memories were just so intense that she was on the edge of breaking up. She hadn't cried since they'd parted company. It was as if all her tears had collected in a pool somewhere deep inside her and had refused to come out.

She cracked a smile. He still had his hand on her arm, but now he released her, raking his fingers through his hair, edgy and awkward.

'What a surprise!' she chirped. 'What brings you back across the ocean?' Before he could see the glimmer of dampness in her eyes, she spun round and began heading to her bike. If he wanted to ask about the landscaping, then he could jolly well do so while they walked.

The silence that greeted her question forced Mia into speech, but her voice was simmering with hostility, even though she was trying so hard to keep a grip on her emotions.

'Has Nat contacted you about my designs for the outside space? You could have emailed me if you had any questions.' They were at her bike now and she circled round it so that they were standing on either side, staring at one another, while she pointedly clutched the handlebars. Let him be in no doubt that she was tired and on her way home, and if he had something to say then he'd better just come right out and say it.

'I haven't come here to ask you about the landscaping.'

'Then what are you doing here?' The smile dropped from her face.

'I came to…talk to you…'

'What about?'

'About us.'

Mia laughed shortly. 'Really? What about us? It's an awfully long way to come to have a conversation about nothing.'

'Is that what you think we are?'

'Yes.' She tilted her chin at a defiant angle. Her eyes stung. 'We said goodbye, Max. What else is there to say?' She began unlocking her bicycle.

'I've had two weeks to think…to miss you…to realise that saying goodbye was the wrong thing for me to do.'

Mia's head shot up and she glared at him with sudden fury. All those little hints and warnings he had dished out rushed at her and she saw red. Talk? He wanted to *talk* about them? Because he'd had a couple of weeks to think, and to miss her, and to realise that saying goodbye had been the wrong thing for him to do…?

Could he be any more arrogant? To assume that he could remind her that he wasn't in it for the long haul because holidays always came to an end, but then, having decided that he might want a bit more of a holiday, maybe a mini-break, assume he was entitled to hop back on a plane, chat her up and… what? She'd fall into his arms and take whatever was on offer?

All the pain and heartbreak she had felt when things had ended between them now surfaced with crippling speed.

'Tough.' She gritted her teeth.

She began cycling off and he began jogging alongside her. She wasn't looking at him, but she was aware of heads turning in their direction. A blistering argument in full throttle was always a captivating sight for curious bystanders.

Annoyingly, he wouldn't give a damn, while she could only wonder if anyone looking at them might know her.

'Go away,' she puffed, gathering pace, while he did likewise.

'Not until we talk.'

He'd dictated the pace and the direction of their intense, short-lived relationship. She'd been so determined not to let that happen, but happen it had, because she'd fallen madly in love with him until bit by bit she'd become the puppet manoeuvred by his all-empowering hand. The only blessing was that she hadn't been idiot enough to show him how she felt. She was sure that, if she had, he wouldn't be running alongside her now telling her that he wanted to pick up where they'd left off.

She'd had plenty of time to make sense of this guy. He was a sensualist who enjoyed a casual acceptance that whatever woman he wanted would dance to his tune. She was sure that, when it came to the relationships he had had in the past, *he* would always have been the one to end them because he would have become bored. Circumstances had dictated that he make a decision about them. He couldn't have remained in Hawaii for ever, so he had walked away. But she thought now, pedalling furiously, he hadn't quite had time to become bored, so he had returned to continue what they had until he *did* become bored. At which point, she would see the dust kicked up by his rapidly departing feet.

Thanks, she thought, but no thanks.

'Okay!' She braked so suddenly that he was still running but he swivelled round, slowed his pace and stood looking at her. He didn't even have the decency to be out of breath. 'Talk! No, let *me* say what you're about to say! All this stuff about your two-week thinking period? I know where you're going, Max.'

'Please let's not have this conversation here, Mia,' was all he said, but there was something about the tone of his voice, the way he was looking at her…

She hesitated, annoyed with herself. There was a café several paces along which looked reasonably quiet, probably because it looked reasonably pricey. She gave a curt nod towards it and headed there.

It was mellow inside. Some of the tables were full, and the area around the bar was busy, but they were still able to grab an empty table to the side where they sat in silence until orders for drinks were given.

Tempted to go for a bracing Maui lager, instead she had a soft drink.

The silence was making her even more edgy. She didn't want to look at him, because she didn't want to be reminded of just how much he had come to mean to her, but it was an effort to sit in stony silence with her eyes averted.

'You were going to tell me that you were a mind reader,' he finally said, quietly. 'I'm willing to bet that you aren't.'

'You came over here because you're not quite through with what we had,' Mia scorned. He had knocked back drink number one, a whisky, in record time, which was alarming. He also couldn't quite meet her eyes. 'Am I heading in the right direction?'

'It's no good trying to pre-empt what you think I'm going to say,' he told her, but in such a low, driven voice that she had to lean forward to catch what he was saying. He ordered another whisky and she couldn't help herself when she said anxiously, 'Why are you drinking so quickly?'

'Dutch courage,' he said with a wry smile.

'Dutch courage? Why would you need Dutch courage? When have you ever been scared of anything? If this is some kind of tactic to get under my skin, it's not going to work!'

'I need Dutch courage because I've never had this kind of conversation before. I've never...felt this need before.'

'I think you're confusing *need* with *lust*.'

'I don't think the two are connected at all, and that's why I'm finding this difficult. I've never felt this way about anyone before. Never thought I could. Just hear me out and, if after you want to walk away, you have my word that I won't follow you. Thing is, Mia, you came at me like a bolt from the blue. One minute I had a plan for my life, and the next minute you'd managed to blow a hole right in the middle of it and I didn't know what the hell had happened.'

Mia shifted uneasily. Something was blooming inside her and she couldn't shove it down where it belonged.

She wanted to hear more. She didn't want to hear more. So she waited in silence.

'I just know that what started off as something simple became more and more complicated with each passing second. You got under my skin and you stayed there. I should have known my life was changing when I realised I didn't want you to leave my bed. I wanted you to fall asleep next to me and wanted you to be the first person I saw in the morning when I woke up.'

'Really?' But there was doubt in her voice.

'Really.' He smiled tentatively, and that was so novel for a man as self-assured as he was that she softened and began to open up, began to let those shoots of hope grow. When he absently took her hand and fiddled with her fingers, she didn't pull back.

'For as long as I can remember,' he confided huskily, 'I've been distrustful of relationships. My parents, as far as I was concerned, sacrificed everything in the name of love. Work…

responsibilities… Me. When they were killed in that plane crash, it seemed just another example of their reckless adventuring which always took precedence over everything else. They should never have gone up. The weather was terrible, but there they were, like a couple of love-struck teenagers, acting with the folly of youth instead of a couple of middle-aged parents with three kids to think about.'

He sighed and pressed his thumbs to his eyes, then he looked at her. 'I vowed to always, always be in control of my life. There was no way I would let anyone get me to a place where I forgot what my priorities were. Security. Stability. Relationships were enjoyable breaks in between the more important things in life, and that worked until I met you.'

'And then what happened?' Mia asked breathlessly.

'Then I met you and I fell in love.'

'You…you what?'

'I fell in love with you, my darling. I had all the symptoms but I failed to recognise the illness. Bad metaphor.' He grinned. 'I was so used to the humdrum monotony of having my feet planted on the ground that I failed to appreciate the joy of being able to fly, which is how you make me feel.'

'Me too,' Mia admitted. She felt tears gathering in the corners of her eyes. 'It was so hard not being able to tell you, knowing that you would run a mile if you had any inkling that I was falling madly in love with you. When we were island-hopping, there was always this tightness inside me because I knew it was going to end and when it did...' She shivered and closed her eyes briefly.

'You didn't say anything.'

'How could I? I was proud. Proud enough to think that I had to walk away with my dignity intact.'

'I didn't realise how much that would hurt.'

'Why...? Why didn't you say something sooner?' Mia couldn't help but ask and he shot her a rueful smile.

'You talked about pride,' he said drily. 'You

don't have a monopoly on that particular emotion. It was more than that, though.'

His voice was thoughtful now. 'I just kept telling myself that I would adjust back to the life I'd always known, kept telling myself that I should be pleased that you'd accepted the inevitable with such…indifference. I shut down all the pain and bewilderment and hurt because, for the first time, I wanted a woman to stop me from walking away and you didn't. I told myself that it was only a matter of time until things returned to normal. On all counts, I was wrong. It just took me a while to figure that out. I've been a fool, my darling, but I came here to set the record straight.'

'I love you,' she said simply.

'I want to do everything right,' he told her solemnly. 'No half-measures. No being scared about what might lie in front of me. There's no room when you love someone for playing games or trying to hang on to control. It's about letting go. I love you, need you and want you to be the one I let go to. For ever. So, my darling Mia, will you marry me and be patient with me while I learn how to be less driven?'

'I think I can handle that.' She laughed and touched the side of his face. Such a dear face.

From cloud nine, the whole world looked like the most wonderful place to be.

'I warn you, you're in for quite a riotous ride with my family,' she said.

'Four sisters… I'm guessing I'm not going to get much of a word in edgeways, especially if they're as wonderfully opinionated as you.'

'Just as opinionated and very noisy. But they're going to be so happy to welcome you into the family, and I guarantee my two brothers-in-law will be whooping at the thought of having another guy in their corner for back-up.'

'I can't wait,' he told her, drawing her towards him and kissing her, well aware of the indulgent, amused looks they were attracting.

'Nor, my wonderful husband-to-be, can I…'

* * * * *

LET'S TALK

Romance

For exclusive extracts, competitions and special offers, find us online:

f facebook.com/millsandboon

📷 @millsandboonuk

🐦 @millsandboon

Or get in touch on 0844 844 1351*

For all the latest titles coming soon, visit millsandboon.co.uk/nextmonth

Want even more
ROMANCE?

Join our bookclub today!